ALLURING AIDEN

A TEAM LOCO NOVEL

AMY SPARLING

ONE

Aiden

My Uber driver gives me a curious look as he pulls up to the address I gave him. I've seen that look before, on pretty much every driver who brings me home from the airport. He's looking at the estate and then back at me, with my unkept hair and dark circles under my eyes and thinking, *do you actually live here or are you going to rob the place?*

"Thanks, man," I say, hopping out of the backseat quickly before he bothers voicing his thoughts. He pops the trunk and I grab my suitcase. On instinct, I'm about to slam the car's trunk down with my right hand, but then I remember I can't. As if the pain isn't enough of a reminder.

My broken wrist hurts like hell.

I drop my suitcase, close the trunk with my good hand, then pick it back up again. I'll be one-armed for the next six weeks if I'm lucky. I've already stayed off my bike for two weeks, which is basically like being in prison. Being unable to ride is probably worse than prison.

Okay, maybe not. Why did I even make that joke? Prison is kind of the whole reason I'm where I am today. I'm Aiden

Strauss, motocross racer. No longer Aiden Strauss, little brother of Mikey Strauss.

Mikey Strauss, otherwise known as the motocross legend.

Former motocross legend.

I let out a sigh, scratch my eyebrow with the hard plaster cast and drag my suitcase toward the front of Strauss Manor.

My parent's house isn't actually called that. It's huge. It's pretty much a mansion. But it doesn't have one of those formal names for it anything. Strauss Manor is what my little sister calls it, and she's almost always being sarcastic when she says it.

My fingers dangle out of the cast, so at least they're somewhat useful. I use one to push the buzzer on the call box just outside the gate that borders the property.

"Hello Mr. Aiden," a cheerful, raspy voice calls over the speaker. I look up into the camera and wave. The speaker box crackles again. "What happened to your arm?" Mr. Ashburn must be in his seventies now, but he's still just as talkative as ever.

"Can I come inside?" I say back. "I'll explain it to you in person."

"Oh, right. Of course."

The black iron gate that keeps strangers out of my parent's estate swings open, the motor whirring next to me. As soon as the gap is wide enough, I slip through with my suitcase in tow.

I gaze up at the Orlando mansion, with its white marble façade and carefully manicured palm trees dotting the cobblestone driveway. This is home. It has been for most of my life.

It just never feels like it.

We moved in here when I was four and my mom was a newly minted trophy wife to the locally famous Allan Strauss, real estate tycoon. Her previous marriage to my worthless father didn't work out, and she took me and Mikey and brought us straight into the good life. She had our last names changed to my step dad's and everything. A year later, my little sister Bella was born. I started kindergarten here. I came home from high school parties here. I was playing pool in the game room when I got the call that I was being offered a spot on Team Loco's professional motocross team.

But it never feels like home.

I have this theory that living in a house too damn big will do that do you. I feel most at home when I'm packed into a hotel room on the road with my teammates. Sitting on my dirt bike waiting for a race to start—that's home.

This mansion? Not home.

But it's the only place I've got and it's where I'll have to spend the next six weeks until I'm healed. My manager, Marcus, told me not to get my hopes up about racing any time soon. Even after my bones are healed, the team's doctor has to clear me for riding, and that'll probably be after a few weeks of PT. All I want to do is get back on my bike, with my real family, Team Loco.

Only six more weeks to go.

The house smells warm and inviting despite the cold feel of the marble flooring and expensive decorations we're never allowed to touch.

Mr. Ashburn greets me in the foyer. He's my step dad's cousin and has been a live-in butler for all of my life. I think he's kind of a loser with nothing else going for him and that's why my step-dad gave him this "job", if it can be called that. All he really does is answer the door and watch TV all day.

"So what happened to your wrist?" he asks.

"Crashed during a race," I say, scowling at the red plaster cast. "I could tell it was broken immediately when I couldn't even pick up my bike. I was winning too, which sucked balls."

He lifts an eyebrow at my choice of words. "Sorry to hear that, son. How long until you're healed?"

"Six weeks," I say, avoiding the whole truth which is that physical therapy will probably take longer. "I'm gonna crash here until then."

"Sounds good," he says. "Need me to carry that to your room?"

I shake my head. Technically it's probably his job, but I've never liked having "the help" help me when I lived here. "I've got it. Thanks, man."

I roll my suitcase to the stairs and then clunk it up each one until I get to the second floor. My room is on the opposite side of the mansion from my parents, right across the hallway from Bella. I miss her like crazy. She's a cool kid—well, teenager. I keep forgetting that she's sixteen now and not a little girl anymore. I toss my suitcase in my room and then knock on her bedroom door.

"Bella!" I call out, waiting for a reply.

I knock again a few seconds later. "Hello? Your brother is home! I need a hug!"

Still nothing.

Frowning, I head down to the game room but there's no one in there, either. I check the movie room and the library and then the kitchen. Nothing.

But I do grab a snack while I'm down here. Looks like Connie is still gainfully employed as the live-in housekeeper because our fridge is filled with fresh guacamole, which was always her specialty.

I take it out and grab some chips, then carry it all outside to the backyard. Bella must be in the pool, enjoying the last few weeks of summer. It's August, and school will start soon.

But our pool is also empty. What the hell? I drop my food on the patio table and fish my phone out from my pocket. There's only ten percent battery left because I watched Netflix on it on the whole flight back home.

I call her, and her phone goes straight to voicemail. Okay, now I'm starting to worry.

I head back inside. "Mom?" I call out, cupping my hands to my mouth. "Allan?"

I wait a beat for a response, but yelling across this house isn't very useful most of the time. No one can hear you. "Mom!" I try again. They're probably not home.

Ever since Bella was old enough to walk, my parents started traveling all the time, leaving us with Connie and Mr. Ashburn. The last few times I've been home, they haven't. Including Christmas and Thanksgiving. Bella and I still had a great time without them, though.

A hear a door open from down the hallway and I walk toward the sound. It's Connie, wearing a black tracksuit with her graying hair pulled into a huge bun on top of her head.

"What's all that yelling for, boy? You scared me!"

"Sorry, Connie," I say, walking into her outstretched arms for a hug.

When I was a kid, she was taller than me, but as the years have gone by, I grew up and she seemed to get shorter. Now, her head fits under my chin.

"Are my parents home? Is Bella home? Is anyone home?"

She chuckles and then sees my arm. "What on earth happened to you?" she says, eyes wide.

"It's nothing. Just a fracture."

She doesn't seem to believe me. "This is a cast, boy. That is serious. Are you okay? Do you need some pain medicine?"

I shake my head. "I'm good. I promise."

I've got a bottle of hydrocodone in my suitcase but I only take it at night. I'm an athlete and I need to stay that way.

"Where's Bella?" I ask again.

She frowns. "Bella?"

"Um yes. My sister?" I really shouldn't have to explain this. Connie *raised* my sister.

"She's not here, Aiden." She puts a hand on my arm. "You knew that, right?"

"Knew what?" I say. The way she looks at me sends a sickening feeling of dread down my spine. If something happened to my sister and no one told me, I will—

"She moved out," Connie says with a chuckle that silences my fears. "Months ago."

"Moved out? She's sixteen years old!"

Connie shakes her head, like I've misunderstood. "She didn't move out on her own, she moved to Louisiana with your grandmother."

I stand here for a second wondering why these words don't make any sense. Our grandmother? She must mean my mom's mom, the crazy old Cajun lady I haven't seen in years. She used to come visit us for holidays when I was a little kid, but she never got along with Allen. She didn't like my mom's new fancy rich lifestyle. To be honest, I kind of forgot that she existed.

"Where are my parents?" I ask.

Connie shrugs. "Aruba, I think? I never know."

"Does Mom know that Bella moved?"

"Of course. She wasn't happy about it, but you know Bella. She does what she wants."

I close my eyes and run my good hand through my hair. The only thing I was looking forward to for the next six weeks was hanging out with my sister. I've barely seen her since I became a pro racer. She used to spend every weekend at the local races with me before Team Loco picked me up. Obviously she couldn't travel the country with us since she was still in school, so she had to stay behind. I miss her. She's my best friend. The only family member I actually like.

"Where's Mikey?" I ask as an afterthought. "Did he move out too?"

"Nah," Connie says, shaking her head. "He's still living here. I think he's out with his girlfriend today."

I don't really care about Mikey. When we were kids, it was just the two of us until Bella came along. He grew up poor with me. He rode dirt bikes with me. He was my idol for a few short years, and then he was arrested for cocaine and spent six months in jail. It was just after he got out that I was signed to Team Loco.

He never even congratulated me.

So screw him.

I take a deep breath. I don't even want guacamole now. This isn't how I expected to come home, to an empty mansion and six weeks of nothingness ahead of me.

Connie tilts her head. "Are you okay? Want me to make you some food?"

"I'm fine," I say. I take my phone and try calling my sister again, but it goes straight to voicemail.

In my bedroom, I feel more like a guest. Someone—my mother probably—has replaced my teenage bedroom furniture with fancy expensive shit that looks like it should be in some model home instead of a guy's room. My TV and clothes and stuff are still here, only it's all been organized and arranged differently. Good thing there's nothing important or private in here.

I drop onto my new bed and turn on the TV, trying to remember the last time I was home. I've been back a few times just to sleep a day or two until my next flight out for another race, but it's been a year since I've actually lived here. I wonder if my other teammates feel so out of place when they go back home.

There's a framed picture on my wall that's new. Mom must

have found it and decided to hang it up. It's me, when I'm about six years old, holding my first trophy. Mikey and I loved dirt bikes but we couldn't afford one until mom's new husband came around. He bought us both bikes as bribery presents so we'd like him. It worked.

My mom and Allen took us to races for a few years and then they got bored and usually pawned it off on Mr. Ashburn until Mikey was old enough to drive us himself. I remember this race. It was the first time I knew for a fact that I wanted to do this for the rest of my life.

I take a picture of it and post it to Instagram, thinking my fans would get a kick out of it. I am not too manly to admit that six year old me was pretty damn cute.

Within seconds, comments start flying in.

Now I regret posting it. Social media is fun when I'm interacting with fellow racers or friends, but the fangirls can sometimes be a bit much.

Daddy!! One of the comments says.

I scroll down and see the same word—*daddy*—another dozen times. I don't get it, the whole daddy thing. I think it's supposed to be sexy but it's just weird to me. Other commenters confess their love for me, complete with emojis.

One says, *when will you just love me back already?!?!?!*

I lift an eyebrow. I'm grateful for my fans. I really am. But sometimes I wish I could tell everyone *not* to love me. They don't know me. I'm just some guy. I'm a skilled racer, and yeah, my physique is good because I work out nonstop. But I'm nothing special.

I haven't even had a girlfriend in years.

TWO

Jenn

IF MY FIRST DAY OF CLASSES HADN'T GIVEN ME A headache, my dad's power tools would do the job just fine. I'm officially a junior at the University of Louisiana Lafayette this year, and my first day of classes was a nightmare. Now that my core classes are done, I finally get to start the good stuff for my degree. Or so I thought. Physical therapy courses aren't easy in the slightest. I'm weighed down with epic paperwork, textbooks, and a stack of one hundred vocabulary words I'm supposed to have memorized in a week.

All I wanted to do after school today was come to work and try to relax. But my dad had other ideas. He's currently standing on the roof of the shop with a chainsaw in his hand. It's so loud it's echoing off the metal walls and driving me crazy.

I finish checking out a customer and then walk outside. Thirty Six Cycles is my dad's motorcycle shop that's located off County Road 36. (I know. He's very creative like that.) The building is long and narrow, with a retail shop up front and mechanic bays in the back where our mechanics work their magic. People come from all over the place to get their bikes worked on here because we have the most skilled employees. In fact, my dad might be the least skilled of everyone.

I hold my hand up to my forehead to block the sun from my eyes. "Dad?" I call out.

He turns off the chainsaw. "Hi, Jenn. What's up?"

"You, apparently," I say. "What are you doing up there?"

"Just trying to get these branches down." He uses the chainsaw to point to the massive oak tree. Its branches are extending out in all directions, some of which are hanging over the roof of the shop.

"It's hurricane season," Dad says. "One snapped branch will go right through the roof."

I roll my eyes. Mom would kill him if she saw him up there. That's about as dangerous as it gets, and my dad isn't known for having good reflexes.

"You should call a professional," I yell out to him.

He shakes his head, waving me off with the hand that's not holding the chainsaw. "I got this, hon. Check it out."

He cranks the motor again and then walks to the edge of the roof, aiming the blades at a large branch that extends about twenty feet from the trunk of the tree.

I want to close my eyes, but instead I get out my phone in case I have to call 911. Dad grips the chainsaw, struggling to get it through the thick branch. I hold my breath.

With a crack, the branch bends and sags, until finally it breaks free. Only instead of making a clean fall to the ground, it crashes into a nearby powerline.

A loud pop snaps through the air, and there's a flash and smoke, and then the lights in the shop go off.

"Uh oh..." Dad says, watching the powerline all curled up around the downed tree branch.

"Would you please get down from there?" I say. "You're going to hurt yourself!"

He grudgingly listens, and once he's back on the ground safely, I give him a look.

"The power's out," I say.

"Yeah... I figured as much..." Dad says, frowning. He scratches his head.

The front door of the shop opens and Rafael, one of our mechanics, jogs outside. "The power is out, Mr. Doherty."

"Oh trust me, we know," I say sarcastically.

Dad chuckles. "I'm gonna go call the power company. You guys can head home early. I don't think this will be fixed anytime soon."

Rafael lets out a little whoop. "Awesome! I think I'll head to the track to ride." He holds the door open for me as we walk back into the shop. "You gonna ride, too?"

I didn't think I'd get to ride all week because of school starting, but he makes a good point. Getting out of work early means there's some unexpected free time. The motocross track is like a second home to me, next to the bike shop. I grew up at both of these places and only ever went home to eat and sleep.

"Yeah," I say after thinking about it for a second. "I think I will go ride."

"Cool," he says, flashing me a smile. "I'll see you there."

Rafael is like me in that we both love to ride but aren't very good at it. I mean, I'm okay. I can hold my own. I'm just not a racer. My dad bought my first dirt bike when I was six and I was so scared of it that it took me a while to be able to ride it around the yard going slower than a lawn mower. But eventually I grew to love dirt bikes.

I've never raced, even though that's kind of what everyone else does. I just go up to the local track and ride for fun on prac- tice days. I love the feel of the wind in my face, the speed of the bike, and the way that everything just blurs right on by when you ride. There's no school work or chores or stresses when you ride. It's just you and the dirt.

I do the best I can at closing up the shop for the day. Without power, I can't shut down the computer or clock out, but I take the money out of the cash register and put it in the zippered bank bag which I lock in the safe in Dad's office. I lock up the front door, smirking when I see Dad out front talking to the power company. He's waving his arms around, no doubt trying to make it seem like something crazy happened to the tree branch instead of what actually happened.

I grab my purse and my keys and send a text to my boyfriend Jay. Unlike me, Jay does race dirt bikes. He's the fastest racer around here, and he wins every single race. He's really bitter about not being picked for a professional motocross team yet, but I always tell him that he's only twenty one and he's got time. He usually disagrees with me, saying that most pro racers start their career right after high school.

I text him that I got out of work early and want to hit up the track, and when he doesn't reply I assume he's already there. Jay spends all his free time at the track. It's admirable how hard he works.

When I finish closing up shop and walk out to the parking lot, my bike is already magically loaded into my truck bed.

I look around and then spot Rafael climbing into his truck. "Did you do this?" I ask.

He grins at me before closing the truck door and cranking his engine. The window rolls down and he leans out, smacking the side of his truck door with his palm. "Last one to the track has to unload the bikes!"

"Not fair!" I say, laughing. I scramble to jump in my truck but he's already driving off.

Rafael is a good guy. He's worked for my dad ever since he graduated high school, and my dad thought he had such a natural talent with bikes that he paid to send him to mechanic school. Now he's in his thirties and married with two twin boys who want to grow up and be just like their dad. It's really cute. Every time I see Rafael and his happy family at the track, I know that's what I want for Jay and me someday. A happy motocross family.

The local motocross track is only a few miles away, which is probably why my dad's shop gets so much business. They're a popular track in the state and everyone who goes there drives by Thirty Six Cycles and eventually stops to get their bikes worked on or to buy race fuel or bike parts.

I pay the twenty bucks to ride and then look for Rafael's truck so I can park next to him. But today's my lucky day, because I see Jay's motorhome instead. Jay only lives half an hour from the track, but he likes to bring his motorhome with him during the hot summer months because he can hook it up to the track's free electricity and have air conditioning. Here on the Gulf Coast, air conditioning is a necessity during the summer.

My headache seems to vanish when I realize he's here. I haven't seen him in a few days and I'm missing him terribly. I've been so stressed over school starting and now all I want is to relax with my boyfriend and get some laps in on the track.

I park my truck next to his motorhome. His bike is here, so he's probably inside cooling off. I check my phone. He hasn't texted me back yet. Weird.

The roar of dirt bikes is louder as I climb out of my truck. There's at least a dozen people out on the track right now, which is pretty busy for a Tuesday. I love that my favorite sport is getting more popular. It's the greatest sport on earth. Not to mention, it has the hottest guys.

I smile to myself as I walk up to Jay's motorhome. I pull open the door and loud music hits me. I guess that's why he didn't text me back. He couldn't hear his phone over all this noise.

I step inside and look around, but he's not sprawling on the couch like usual.

"Babe?" I say, walking toward the bedroom part of the tiny motorhome. The curtain is pulled back. Shit, I hope he didn't get hurt and come back here to rest it off.

"Babe?" I say again, pulling back the curtain.

Jay is here, but he's not hurt.

He's balls deep in another woman. They don't even notice me at first. They keep going it at for a few seconds, long enough for me to realize that the slut my boyfriend is banging is Miranda Brown, who has the nickname Track Ho for a reason. She's been hooking up with every guy she can get her disgusting hands on ever since before we graduated high school.

My entire world seems to blur and then shatter before my eyes. Jay and I have been together for three years. We're perfect together. We're happy.

Or so I thought.

My voice feels strangled, but I mange to say something. "What. The. Hell."

Now they can hear me. Jay jumps and turns around, eyes wide like a rodent that's been caught digging in the trash. And honestly, digging in trash is what he's doing right now.

"Oh shit," he says. There's so much emotion behind that word—I can't tell if he's embarrassed or ashamed or pissed off.

I can feel tears lingering in my eyes, waiting to be unleashed, but the second I lock eyes with Miranda, fury takes their place. She's grinning.

Grinning.

The bitch.

She's wanted my boyfriend forever, just like she wants every guy who is even remotely talented at motocross. She doesn't even ride bikes herself. She just rides the riders.

I'm going to be sick.

"Jenn," Jay finally says after ten painful seconds of silence. Again, I can't tell the emotion behind his voice. You'd think he would start pleading with me, giving me those clichéd lines of *it's not what it looks like.*

I shake my head. I don't want to hear it. I don't want to keep seeing it.

I just want to be out of here.

I turn on my heel and race out of the motorhome, slamming the door closed behind me. I jump back in my truck and take off, not caring that I just wasted twenty dollars to ride. I can't seem to care about anything right now.

All I know is that I am never dating a motocross guy again.

THREE

Aiden

When I wake up, it takes me a second to remember where I am. I'm not always home very often, but this has never happened before. Probably from the new furniture in my room and the fact that I now wake up in immense pain in my right wrist. I must have tossed and turned a lot to make it hurt this bad.

I sit up and reach for last night's bottled water off the shiny new nightstand. I down a pain pill and then reach for my phone.

Luckily, my sister's phone rings this time when I call her instead of going straight to voicemail like yesterday.

"Bro," she answers with a smile in her voice. She calls me Bro when she's being a goofball. "What's up?"

It's good to hear Bella's voice again. My mom and step-dad have never been very lovey-dovey parents and my older brother Mikey hasn't been much of a brother to me since right before he got arrested. Back then I was finally getting fast enough to challenge him on the track and he didn't like that. Mikey was born with a natural motocross talent. I had to work for mine.

But Bella has always been my sweet little sister. She's the sane one of the family.

"I'm just sitting here at home," I tell her. "And I'm wondering where you are."

"I'm at home."

"No, you're not," I say.

She snorts. "I'm at *my* home. Grandma's is home to me now."

My wrist is killing me, so I fall back in bed. "Since when did you decide to move there? We barely saw her when we were growing up."

Bella's voice softens. "I don't know, Aiden. Grandma and I are pen pals. I used to write to her all the time and she would write back. So I guess I'm just closer to her than anyone else in the family."

"Wow...I can't believe I didn't know that."

"There's a lot you don't know," she says. Her voice is a little sadder than normal. "You're always gone. That's why I left. I got sick of being stuck in that huge house with Mikey and his gross girlfriend. Mom and Dad are never home and I'm just sick of it."

"What about school?" I say. Bella has gone to the same Orlando private school her entire life.

"I quit," She says simply. "Mom was pissed, but whatever. I homeschool myself online now. It's through a state college and it's really cool because I get college credit for my AP classes."

"Wow," I say again. My sixteen year old sister is all grown up. She's doing stuff on her own now. And part of the reason she left is because of me. "I'm sorry, Bells. I should have come home more often."

"It's not your fault," she says. "I'm proud of you. You're living your dream as a fancy professional motocross guy. All my friends think you're super hot."

I chuckle. "They don't want me now. I'm broken and worthless."

"Wait, what?"

"You didn't hear?"

"Oh my god, Aiden, what happened?" My sister shrieks.

I have to admit, it feels good to have someone care about me. Lately I feel like my only worth is to Team Loco and if I'm broken then I'm worth nothing. I tell her about how I broke my wrist racing and now I'm benched for at least six weeks but probably longer.

"Aiden!" Bella chastises better than my mom does. "You should have told me sooner!"

"It just happened," I say quickly. "About a week ago. I spent some time with the guys since I couldn't race but then I decided to come home and focus on healing. I can't be travelling every week for no reason. But now I'm home and the one person I wanted to see is in Cajun town."

"Hey, Cajun food is amazing," Bella says with a laugh. "Do you want to come stay with Grandma and me?"

The only thing I remember about the very few trips we took to Louisiana in my childhood was that it's hot as hell and boring as hell. But I look around my room in this house and realize there's nothing going for me here, either. I miss my sister.

"Is there room for me? Would Grandma mind?"

"There's tons of room. Grandma has a four bedroom house. I mean, it's nothing like Mom and Dad's manor, but it's cool. She's on like twenty acres of land in this small town called Breaux Valley and I like it here. It's not crazy like Orlando."

"And what about Grandma? Would she mind?"

"Bro, she would love to see you. She loves all of us. Except maybe Mom who she's mad at because she never calls or visits. But come over. Get a flight here, like today."

I grin and look around my room. All the important stuff I

own is still packed in my giant suitcase and all I have to do is throw in my phone charger and bottle of pills and I'm ready to hit the road.

"I'll text you when my flight lands," I say.

She lets out a squee of excitement. "Can wait to see you, Aiden!"

"Me too," I say.

BELLA SEEMS EVEN SHORTER than I remember. Her long brown hair has been cut into a shoulder length style. She jumps up and down, waving at me from across the terminal at this small Louisiana airport. It feels good to have someone excited to see me. For the last year my whole life has been motocross. Races and practice and working out. The other guys on Team Loco have become my best friends and my new family, but let's face it—we're just a group of guys who race motocross. We're not a mushy-feelings type of family. And while I'm manly as hell on the race track, sometimes you just need a long bear hug from your sister.

"I missed you, kid," I say, wrapping my arms tightly around her.

"I missed you more," she says, her voice all muffled from being squished against my chest. When we finally pull away, she smiles up at me. She does seem happier than ever now that she's here instead of being cooped up at our parent's house.

"You're my favorite family member," she says.

"You're mine," I say back. "Can we get some food on the way home, I'm freaking starving."

She laughs and takes me outside to the parking area. "Yeah we can eat. Cajun food!"

I roll my eyes. Bella stops in front of an older model Ford Taurus. It's white, with chipped paint and missing hubcaps. I lift an eyebrow because there's no way she's about to get inside of this thing—but yes, she does.

She opens the driver's side door and slides into the ancient car. It's at least twenty years old. I pop open the passenger door and lean in.

"Are you serious? This is *seriously* your car?"

She rolls her eyes and starts the engine. I put my stuff in the backseat and then sit up front next to her. "Why would you drive this POS when our parents would be happy to buy you a new car?"

She bites her bottom lip and gives a little shrug.

"Well?" I say. "It's his Grandma's car or something?" It certainly looks like an old lady's car.

She sighs. "Apparently you haven't talked to Mom."

"Not really," I say. "I mean she comments on my Instagram every now and then but I can't remember the last time we talked." My mom seems like she spent her whole life waiting for her kids to be grown so she could go live a life without them. Like I said, we aren't very touchy feely family.

Bella pulls onto the main road, which isn't saying much because we're surrounded by trees and empty land. "When I left I told them I didn't want their help anymore. I said all they do is throw money at me and I didn't want it. I wanted a relationship with them or nothing at all."

"Holy shit," I say. "That was bold."

She snorts. "Mom decided to cut me off financially to prove a point or something... So.. no car for me. Grandma lets me drive her car."

I scrunch up my nose. "Bella, I'll buy a car for you."

"It's fine." She adjusts the air vent to where it's blowing on her but the air isn't exactly cold. I'm already beginning to sweat, which is going to make my cast itchy as hell. "I'm fine sharing a car with Grandma."

I give her a look. She shrugs. "Seriously, I'm fine."

"I think we should buy you a car," I say. "Something safer at least. It doesn't even have to be fancy but I can't have you –or Grandma for that matter—driving such a clunker."

"Grandma doesn't drive much." Bella glances over at me. "But... there is this one car..."

"Where?"

"It's a used car and it's ten thousand dollars."

"How used?" I ask.

"Not very. It's like five years old."

"I'd rather get you a new car. Something safe and reliable."

"This is a reliable car, I promise. Mr. Doherty checked it out before putting it up for sale and he owns a mechanic shop and everything and said he'd give a warranty on it."

I can't help but smirk. "If you're so happy with driving this piece of shit, why do you know all this information about this other car?"

She grins. "Well... I was hoping to save up enough money to buy it myself. But it'll probably sell soon. It's a nice car and it's priced right and everyone trusts Mr. Doherty." She wiggles her eyebrows. "It's a Camaro."

"I'm sold. Let's go get it."

She shakes her head. "No... I can't take your money, Aiden. I've got four thousand saved up and I was thinking of asking him to do a payment plan for me."

"Just let me buy it."

"I can't take your money, Aiden."

"Why not?" I say. "I have barely any bills and no girlfriend to spend my money on. I get paid pretty well with Team Loco so just let me do this for you. I love you, sis. I want to do something nice for you."

Her shoulders fall, but I can tell in the way she presses her lips together that she's trying to hide a smile. She's going to relent, I can tell. "Fine..." she says, her lips splitting into a grin.

"Whoop," I say, smacking the dashboard of this ugly car. "I am an amazing big brother."

"Don't go getting a big head," she says. "You weren't even there for my last birthday!"

"But I sent you that new MacBook," I say.

She grins. "That was a pretty badass present. Plus it's okay that you're gone all the time because my friends think it's awesome that I'm related to you." She bats her eyelashes and makes her voice all high pitched. "Oh my God, Aiden is soooo hot, Bella! You have to introduce me to him!"

"Your friends are too young for me, but I'm flattered."

She slows down and puts her blinker on as we approach a large building called Thirty Six Cycles.

"They have a bike shop out here?" I ask.

"They have a dirt bike track here too," she says, pointing to the road in front of us even though I can't see anything. "It's about three miles that way. I drive past it every day getting to Grandma's. That's why all my new Louisiana friends are obsessed with you because they live in a motocross town."

"Cool," I say. I wouldn't mind stopping by this track some-time. Just because I can't ride doesn't mean I have to stay away. Being at a track, surrounded by exhaust fumes and loud motors is my favorite place in the world.

Bella parks next to a shiny black Camaro that's facing the main road with a For Sale sign on the windshield. It's a pretty nice car, and seems to be in great shape. Not a scratch on it and the interior is clean and well-maintained. It smells like girly shampoo in here which tells me that a girl probably owned it.

"Hey there, Bella," a middle-aged man says as he approaches us. "Back for another look?"

"This is my brother," Bella says, motioning to me.

The man's eyes light up in recognition. "No shit! Aiden Strauss in the flesh! Good to meet you boy." He goes to shake my hand but I hold up my cast.

"Sorry, I'm out of order."

"Aww, man, what a shame. How long are you out for?"

"Six weeks," I say with a sigh.

He claps me on the back. "Well, you'll get back out there before you know it. I'm a big fan of Team Loco. It's really nice to meet you."

"Guess what, Mr. Doherty," Bella says. She's bouncing on the balls of her feet. "Aiden is going to buy this car for me."

Mr. Doherty beams. "All right. Wonderful! Jenn will be excited that the car is going to you. She specifically told me not to sell it to some asshole."

Bella grins. "I told her I was going to do everything I could to buy it."

He leads us inside the motorcycle shop and says something about us arriving at the right time because the power was recently restored. He says he'll go get the title and paperwork and meet us back here in a minute. I breathe in the smell of the bike shop, all rubber and oil and new gear. I love it.

"Come on," Bella says, tugging my good arm toward the front of the store. "I gotta tell Jenn the good news."

Jenn must be the girl behind the counter. She hasn't looked up at us yet, but I can tell from here that she's beautiful. One of those girls that are born just naturally stunning. She has long light brown hair and sexy pink lips. My eyes are drawn to her lips as we approach the front counter. She's staring at her phone and she seems sad. But damn, is she sexy as hell. Even under her black T-shirt I can tell she's got curves in all the right places.

And what's better than anything is that she's clearly older than my sister. She's around my age for sure.

Bella rushes up to the girl and tells her the good news. She smiles back, but it doesn't reach her eyes. There's definitely something bothering this girl.

"My brother is buying your car," Bella says, looking back at me.

That's when Jenn also meets my gaze. Her eyes widen for a second, the recognition dawning on her just like it did with Mr. Doherty. To most people on the planet, I'm just some guy. But to people connected with the motocross world, I'm a professional racer. Being kind of famous never gets old.

Sometimes the only thing that gets me through lonely nights of being single is hitting up my social media and seeing all the dirty photos random girls send me. I don't exactly get off on them, but the attention feels nice.

I haven't been with a girl in forever, and the tightness in my pants right now is making me uncomfortable.

Jenn nods once at me. "Nice to meet you."

"Same," I choke out. Damn. I need to get my shit together. She's just some gorgeous girl that I'll never see again after my wrist is healed. Yet I can't stop picturing kissing those perfect lips.

Luckily, Mr. Doherty comes back with paperwork and kills my boner instantly. It helps if I don't look at Jenn anymore. I write a check for the car and he signs the title over to me, and then we're on our way. Bella is so excited she can't stand it as we walk out to her new car.

"Ah, damn." I say with a sigh. "This means I have to drive the shitty Taurus back to Grandma's."

She laughs and tosses me the keys. "Yup!"

"How much further until we're at Grandma's?" I ask.

"Only about five minutes," Bella says. "Then we can say

hello to Grandma, drop off your stuff, and go for a ride in my new car!" Her eyes narrow mischievously. "Or... we could come back here."

"Why would we do that?" I say.

She gives me a knowing grin. "So you can flirt with Jenn."

I do my best impression of acting like I have no idea what she's talking about. "You're insane."

She laughs. "I saw the way you looked at her! But you might as well get over it because she totally has a boyfriend. It's this guy named Jay and they've been together for a few years."

Damn. I try not to let it show, but that sucks. Not that I would admit it to Bella, but it had crossed my mind to come back here and flirt with Jenn. I'm so off my game that I have no idea how to talk to a girl. But Jenn was sexy enough to make me try.

I guess that idea is pointless now.

FOUR

Jenn

Dad holds up the check as if looking at it from a different angle somehow makes it better. "Can you believe it?" he says, beaming at the small piece of paper. "I'm holding an autograph from Aiden Strauss! That's pretty cool."

I yank it away from him. "Too bad it's going straight to the bank."

My dad is so starstruck that he might not even cash the check if it belonged to him. Unfortunately for him, it was my car we just sold and I'm keeping the money. It's going toward paying off my new truck.

Dad frowns. "I should have asked for his autograph on something else."

Dad has worked in this motocross world for over twenty years and you'd think he'd be used to it by now. But anytime the rare event happens when someone even mildly famous comes to the shop, he gets all excited like he's a kid on Christmas morning. I know Aiden's sister Bella from around town. She's still in high school but it's a small town so it's hard not to know everyone here. I've seen her at the track before and sometimes we take walks together at the local park. I'll try to see if I can ask her to get her brother to sign something for my dad and I'll give it to him for his birthday. He'd probably freak out.

I smile a little at the thought, and then tuck the check away in my purse for safe keeping. I'm glad I sold my old car but I still have to work until closing, so I can't take it to the bank yet.

Dad gets a call and heads into his office and I ring up a purchase for a lone customer. Once the customer pays, he walks out the door, leaving the shop in silence except for a distant hum of one of the mechanic's drills.

It's too quiet. All the thoughts I've been trying to keep at bay come flooding back to me when it's quiet. It hasn't even been a whole twenty-four hours since the worst day of my life.

It feels so much longer though. I haven't slept. I've barely eaten. I'm surprised no one has said anything about how shitty I look today, but I'm grateful for it nonetheless. I don't want any attention. I don't want anyone asking about what's got me so sad.

My boyfriend is a cheater.

That's the worst part. It's not just that we're over, that my three-year relationship that I'd thought was going so well is just ripped in half and tossed on a burning pile of memories. No. It's not that it's over.

It's that he cheated.

With Miranda Brown.

My lip curls just thinking about her. Of all the women in the world, he slept with her. Gross.

It dawns on me that I need to get an STD test immediately. I have no idea how long he's been unfaithful, and if *anyone* is covered with STDs, it's that bitch Miranda.

I let out a long sigh and run my hand over my face. This is not how I expected my junior year of college to go. This isn't at all part of the plan. A week ago, I was entertaining the idea that

Jay might propose to me before my next birthday. Now, I am single.

The rest of the workday is pretty slow. We get a few customers, but mostly I'm just standing here trying not to cry. I reorganize the shelves and restock inventory and do everything I can think of to stay busy and keep my mind off Jay. But every time I look at my phone, I'm thinking of him. I changed my phone wallpaper last night, so at least I don't have to see his stupid face anymore. But the sheer lack of notifications on my phone is making this really hard.

Jay hasn't called me or texted me. He hasn't reached out on social media. He hasn't even bothered saying he's sorry.

I guess it doesn't matter. It's not like I want to talk to him. But still. We were together three years. I guess that meant nothing to him.

I sink my head in my palm and lean against the front counter, my gaze going out the window. I see the road, and the place where my old Camaro used to sit before we sold it. I'm glad Bella got the car. I know she wanted it pretty badly.

I'm sure all my friends at the motocross track would think it's pretty cool that Aiden Strauss bought my car, but I don't even feel like calling anyone up to talk about it. Who cares. He's just some famous guy.

And he's gorgeous, way hotter than he looks online. That's saying something because he looks like a damn snack online. But I couldn't even enjoy the eye candy when he was in the shop because all I kept thinking was that a guy like that probably cheats on his girlfriends, too. Motocross guys can't be trusted. The faster they are, the more notoriety they gain in the racing world, the more they can't be trusted. Women throw themselves at guys like that. That's why I don't care that I met the famous Aiden Strauss or that he bought my car.

He's probably a scumbag just like Jay.

Somehow I make it through my shift at work, and then I'm finally driving home. I don't bother asking Rafael if he's going riding tonight. It's perfect weather for it, but I'm not in the mood to see my dirt bike. I don't want to see the track. I don't want to run into Jay.

I hate that he's doing this, breaking my heart and taking away my favorite sport at the same time. I hate it. I hate *him*.

I drive home without music. I'm so caught up in my heartache that I forget to turn it on. Soon, I'm pulling into the driveway of my garage apartment and cutting the engine and dashing inside so I can finally cry all the tears I've been holding back all day.

I'm so glad I live out here, away from my parents. I spent my first two years of college in the dorms, which sucked. But now that I'm a junior, I wasn't required to be on campus but I also didn't want to move back home with my parents because I felt like I'd grown used to being independent and I wanted to stay that way.

But the problem with a small town like Breaux Valley is that there's no apartment complexes. Barely any rental properties. If I wanted to stay in my hometown, close to work and the dirt bike track, I'd need to figure something out. I didn't have enough money to buy a house, and Jay had said he didn't feel right living together before we were officially engaged, so I couldn't move in with him.

A sick feeling shudders through me at the thought. That was just four months ago that we'd had the conversation. Jay's been renting a house in town from his uncle and it has three bedrooms and plenty of space. I'd mentioned moving in and he shut me down. Now I guess I know why. He was probably never planning on proposing to me.

Anyhow, my dad got the brilliant idea to turn the garage into an apartment. It's a two-story building that's set off at the edge of my parent's property. It has its own driveway and everything. The upstairs had always been one massive rec room with a bathroom. Over the summer, we renovated it to be a studio apartment. The only rent I have to pay is the cost of the property taxes and insurance, which is pretty cheap.

Thank God I have my own place right now. I cry the second I walk inside. I drop onto my couch and hold the throw pillow against my chest and just let it all out. The pain and the betrayal and the anger. Because of *all* people, Jay cheated on me with that whore. I hate her. I hate him.

They deserve each other.

After a long time of crying, I feel like I've cried all I possibly can. I sit up and dry my eyes and place a hand over my chest just to feel my heartbeat. I don't feel very sad anymore. I'm mostly just pissed off.

I'm pissed at my cheating ex-boyfriend, but I'm also pissed at myself. How could I have been so stupid? Here I was thinking we were this amazing couple who was happy and in love, and really it was nothing like that.

I stand up and take a deep breath. I tell myself to move on and get over it. To be a woman. To be strong.

I don't need that asshole in my life.

My phone rings. It's probably my mom calling to invite me to dinner like she does almost every night. I decide to tell her I'm sick so I can get out of it. It's halfway true, since I am sick in a way.

But Jay's number flashes on my phone instead of my mom's. I stare at it while it rings, two, three, four times.

It took him long enough.

But I don't answer.

I'm a little ashamed at how long I stare at the phone, wondering if he's going to leave a voicemail. He doesn't.

I set the phone down and then look at the framed photo of

us on the end table. I pick it up, frame and all, and throw it in the trash. Then I peel the photos off the refrigerator, and the walls, and on my nightstand. I get rid of all of them.

I remove the cell phone case he bought for me for Christmas and toss it in the garbage. I go through my closet, taking the shirts that remind me of him, the black lace bra he bought for me, and the bottle of perfume he likes the most.

I throw them all away.

Tears slip down my cheeks, but it feels cathartic to dismantle my whole apartment. Anything he bought me over the last three years goes straight in the trash.

An hour later, my apartment is a little less decorated, but it's a lot better off. I feel clean. I feel new again.

I am no longer a part of a couple. I am just me.

When my phone rings again just after six o'clock, dread rises in my stomach again, but the caller is from a number I don't know.

"Hello?" I answer, taking great care to sound like I haven't been crying.

"Hello, I'm calling for Jenn Doherty."

"This is she," I say.

The female voice on the other line perks up. "This is Blithe with the LaValle Fitness and Physical Therapy Center, and I wanted to let you know that we've selected you for an internship this semester. Are you still interested in the position?"

I feel like screaming out of sheer joy, but somehow I keep my composure. "Yes, absolutely. I would love that."

"Wonderful! You can start this week if your schedule allows, and I'll send you all the information via email."

Once we hang up, I do a little dance in my living room. I got the internship. I got it. Not just any one of the dozen I applied to, but the one I really wanted. LaValle is here in town, so it's not far away. I can intern there on the days I'm not in class and I can work part-time at the shop on the weekends. For most of my life I've known I wanted to be a physical therapist. Now I'm one step closer.

And, I think as I stop dancing and allow a smile to wash out the sadness I've felt for so long now, having an internship, a job, and classes makes for a busy schedule.

There's no time to be heartbroken when you're busy.

FIVE

Aiden

I never thought I'd say this, but my grandma is actually cool. Mom always made it seem like she was some old hag who hated us, but in my three days here I know that's the opposite. Grandma is only sixty-eight years old, so she's not even as old as I had thought she was. She's vibrant and cheerful and spends a lot of time in her garden. She likes to talk about her late husband, the grandfather I never met. She really seems to love my sister and now me. She tells me at least three times a day that I'm welcome here as long as I'd like to stay.

Despite the love and abundance of home cooked meals, it's boring here, out in the boondocks in the middle of swampy Louisiana, and I could see myself getting restless if I had to live here full time.

But for now, a few days of relaxing and hanging with my sister has been pretty great. My stress is gone, and my arm doesn't hurt too much if I just lounge around binge-watching TV shows all day.

Of course, I miss motocross. I miss it a lot. When I'm not broken, I'm riding six days a week, racing once a week, and spending all my free time with the guys on my motocross team. We travel to a new city each week during racing seasons, and right now I'd be in Nevada with the guys if I was still racing.

I've been staying off social media lately because if I get on there, I'll see Team Logo's posts and I'll get depressed that I'm not there. But I was the dumbass who lost control of my bike and got my wrist broken. This six weeks of time out is my own damn fault.

On Friday morning, I wake up to the smell of sausage and pancakes. Grandma is watching the news on a little television in the kitchen while she cooks a mound of food that could feed a small army.

"Looks good," I say, yawning as I enter the yellow kitchen. It's the best room in the whole house, painted brightly and decorated with fresh flowers from Grandma's garden. Plus the whole back wall is made of floor to ceiling windows that look out into the backyard. You can even hear birds chirping in the mornings. It's some peaceful shit. Way better than waking up in a hotel room.

"Morning, Love," Grandma says. She calls Bella and me that. She gives me a plate and starts piling food on it. All the favorites—grits, sausage, eggs, bacon, and toast.

I kiss her on the cheek and then take my plate to the dining table that faces the backyard.

Bella saunters in a few minutes later and pours herself a cup of coffee, adding a ton of creamer and sugar to it. She grabs a slice of toast and takes a bite before dropping into the chair next to me.

"You're gonna get fat," she says, taking one look at my overflowing plate.

"I already am," I say, patting my stomach. I'm slowly losing my six pack since I haven't worked out in two weeks.

My sister snorts. "You're not even close to being fat."

"A good breakfast never hurt anyone," Grandma says, joining us at the table with her own plate of food.

After breakfast, and then lunch, I can't stop thinking about what Bella said. I'm not exactly worried about getting fat, but I do need to do something to maintain as much endurance and fitness as I can while I'm out of motocross. I can't just sit around and watch TV all day or I'll lose all my strength. I'll get back on the bike and won't be able to keep up with the guy in last place.

The sheer thought of that happening lights a fire under me. I've never been hurt like this, not in my entire racing career. I've only had a few bruised ribs and sprained ankles. I can't just sit around and slack.

I have to stay in shape.

I sit up on the couch and look over at my sister, who is half watching the TV show and half playing on her phone. "I need to work out."

She shrugs one shoulder. "Go for a jog or something."

I consider it, but with this heat and humidity, a jog would make my arm sweat so much under the cast. It'd be itchy and gross. I curl my lip.

"I need a gym. Is there a gym around here?"

This small town doesn't even have a McDonald's, so I'm not expecting there to be anything good within an hour's drive. At best, I might be able to order some weight lifting equipment online and have it delivered here, but that doesn't come close to having a professional gym.

"Actually," Bella says, tapping her phone to her cheek while she thinks. "There is a gym. It's not too far from here."

I look it up online and feel a rush of adrenaline when I realize it's just a couple of miles away from Grandma's house. It's open until midnight every day of the week, which means there's no excuse to let my body fall out of shape over the next six weeks.

"Can I borrow your car?" I ask.

Bella frowns. "How are you supposed to work out with a broken arm?"

I stand up from the couch and stretch. "Easy. Legs, abs, back, one arm. Also I can jog. There's no reason the rest of me can't stay fit while my wrist heals."

She rolls her eyes. "This is why girls are in love with you, you know."

"Because I'm a hard worker?"

She smirks. "I guess that's part of it. But it's the *muscles*, Aiden. That's all my friends care about."

"Like I said, your friends are too young for me," I say sarcastically. She tosses me her car keys and I find some workout clothes in my suitcase.

Bella had some friends over the other day. I saw the way they looked at me. It was just the way so many other girls look at me. Lustful. Dreamy. They're falling for what I look like and they don't even know me. I could be a total prick and half of these women wouldn't care, so long as I looked good standing next to them for Instagram photos.

Maybe that's what keeps me single. Unlike some guys I know who are more than happy to hook up with every walking pair of boobs that looks his way, I've never been like that. My teammate Zach used to have a different girl on his arm every weekend until he met Bree and decided he was going to settle down.

I just can't do that—one night stands. It feels gross to me. First, there's the whole threat of catching some disgusting disease from sleeping around, and that's not even all of it. Secret babies from girls whose names you don't remember. Messy breakups when someone gets attached. Waking up next to a stranger whose name you can't even remember. Why do guys get off on this one-night stand thing?

I'd rather be in a relationship with one woman. I'd want to be like my buddy Jett, who found Keanna and knew she was the one for him. They even found a way to make it work with his crazy race schedule and traveling. Keanna is a cool chick. She joins Jett at a lot of the races when she's not busy with school.

I want a relationship like that. But I've never had it. I've never even come close to it.

I climb in Bella's new car which already has my sister's touches added to it. She's put a sticker of her high school mascot on the back window, and there's a high school parking permit on the rear view mirror. But it still smells good in here, like it did the day we bought it. Like cupcakes, and shampoo. It must be what Jenn smells like all the time.

I crank the engine and head toward the main road, remembering the easy directions to this local gym. I decide to stop thinking about girls and relationships. As long as I'm on Team Loco, mildly famous and covered with rippling muscles that I bust my ass to make, I won't be getting a girlfriend.

I could get laid, sure. But not a girlfriend. Every woman who flirts with me now is doing it for one reason. Because I'm famous. They don't know me. They don't care to know me. And I don't have the time to know them, either.

I need to focus on my career. Girls would only get in the way of that. I tell myself that the loneliness I feel each night is just me being pathetic.

At the gym, I walk into a newer building which is a little surprising since everything in this tiny ass town is old. It's called LaValle Fitness and Physical Therapy, and I follow the arrow that says the gym is to the left. The doors to the right go to a PT center. That's kind of good luck on my part, because I'll need physical therapy after my cast is removed. Maybe I'll just stay here and do that instead of going back to Orlando. I sign up for a gym membership, and the guy who works here is about twice as ripped as I am. There's no doubt in my mind that he's on steroids, but whatever. I'm contractually obligated to be healthy and stay off anything like that. I'll never be that bulky, but I don't really want to be.

Lean muscle makes you a faster rider. Bulk would only weigh me down.

There are exactly two people in the gym, and both of them are elderly. One older man is working with a woman who wears scrubs, and I realize the physical therapy section of the gym also merges with the workout section.

I hit the weight machines and do some leg work first. The burn in my hamstrings feels good. It's been way too long. I'm a little out of shape, but soon I'm back in my groove and feeling amazing. I focus on legs, back, and shoulders. Then, a couple hours later, I'm still not ready to go home yet, so I do some arm work with my good arm. If I stay in shape, I'll only have to work hard on my right arm once the cast is off.

I'm in my own world, doing my own thing for so long that I don't even notice when the gym gets a little busier. Several women jog on treadmills and I can feel them staring at me, probably wondering who the new guy is.

Then I see her.

She's wearing a pair of navy blue scrubs and still manages to look sexy even in shapeless clothing. Her light brown hair is pinned back from her face, and she's smiling at another woman in scrubs. She must work here, too.

Damn, a girl with two jobs? Ambition is sexy. No wonder she's already taken.

My chest tightens at the thought of it, and I tell myself to get over it. Why should I care that Jenn has a boyfriend? I don't even know her. I just know how amazing she smells every time I get in that car I bought from her.

I leave the weight machine I was on, in search of something

farther away so I won't be tempted to look at her like some kind of ogling creep. At eight o'clock, almost every employee goes home for the night except the guy at the front counter. The physical therapy part must be closed. There's only a few guys here working out, and one lone woman on a treadmill at the end of the gym. I look around while I'm on the stair climber, and then I see her.

She walks into the women's locker room wearing her scrubs, and then emerges a few minutes later, a towel wrapped around her body. I can see some kind of straps on her shoulders, so she's probably wearing a bathing suit, although my first thought is to picture her naked under that towel.

She doesn't notice me as she walks toward a glass door that leads to the indoor pool. But she takes a right. That door leads to an indoor hot tub. I haven't seen it yet, but the guy who signed me up for membership told mc about it. My membership includes access to the pool, hot tub, and sauna as well.

A hot tub sounds damn good on my aching leg muscles.

I turn off the stair climber and look at my cast, wondering if I could wrap a towel around it to protect it from the bubbles of the hot tub.

Only one way to find out.

SIX

Jenn

My new internship is amazing. The people are nice, and the clients are nice, and I get free access to the gym as well. I've always enjoyed working at my dad's shop since I practically grew up there, but this is different. Here, I'm surrounded by people who share my same interests. It's not all dirt bikes all the time. I get to help people here.

Even after one day as an intern, I'm confident that I'm choosing the right career path. It sucks that it takes so many years in college to be a physical therapist, but it'll be worth it.

Once my shift is over at eight, everyone else goes home, but I've been dying to try out the gym's hot tub. It's massive, and enclosed in a private room next to the sauna. I saw it when I first got here and I've been dreaming about it all day. I've been so stressed with school and now with Jay ripping my heart out, and all I want to do is relax.

I slip into my bathing suit and venture into the hot tub room, hoping it's empty. It is.

Smooth jazz music plays over some hidden speaker and the smell of lavender sets my mind at ease. I step into the hot tub slowly, letting the scorching water soothe my muscles.

I sink down into the bubbles, keeping everything but my head submerged. The water feels amazing. I close my eyes and start to cry.

I don't mean to. My body just takes over the second I feel even slightly relaxed. All the heartache and pain I've been ignoring while I'm busy during the day always crawls back to the surface as soon as things get quiet.

I let the tears roll down my face. I'm over Jay. At least I'm trying to be. My body hasn't quite caught up yet.

A rush of cool air slips into the room along with the sound of a door opening. Shit. I splash water on my face to hide the tears. There's barely any people at the gym this late and I was hoping to have the room all to myself for a while longer.

I glance back.

It's Aiden.

"Oh, sorry," he says, making this confused face. Something in the way he lifts his eyebrows makes me think that he's not really sorry. Like maybe he's faking something.

"You mind if I join you?"

"Go for it." I shrug. "It's a pretty huge hot tub."

Aiden peels off his shirt and wraps it around the red cast on his right arm. I swallow and avert my eyes. Aiden has the kind of six-pack abs that Jay has been wanting for years. My first thought is to ask him how he does it, but then I quickly remember that I'm no longer Jay's girlfriend. I don't have to ask questions for him anymore.

In fact, I hope Jay never gets his abs to look this good.

Aiden sits across from me in the hot tub. It's so large that I bet we couldn't get our feet to touch if we tried. Still, I feel a little cramped in here, as if all my emotions are floating around, making the air thick. I hope he didn't see me crying before I saw him. Luckily, my heart is pounding too hard to want to cry now.

Aiden runs a wet hand through his hair. He exhales slowly,

his eyes closing as the bubbles roll all around him, concealing everything from his chest down. Not that I'm checking him out.

But I'm kind of checking him out.

He tips his head back and is silent for a moment. Since he can't see me, I can't seem to stop checking him out. I don't know why. Maybe it's just interesting, being this close to a motocross celebrity. I bet every dirt bike girl I know would be freaking out if I told them what I was doing right now.

It's too bad I didn't bring my phone with me or I might try to sneak a picture just to make everyone jealous.

"Damn, I wish this cast was off," Aiden says after a long moment of silence. He lifts his head and gives me a flat lipped smile, before turning his gaze to the cast, which is covered in his T-shirt.

"I'm not sure a shirt makes that waterproof," I say.

He chuckles. "I'm improvising. I'll bring a bag next time and some duct tape. I didn't even know there was a hot tub when I got here. This place is sweet."

"I didn't either," I say. I lucked out and had a bathing suit in my truck."

"How long have you been working here?"

"It's my first day. And I'm technically an intern."

He seems impressed. "Oh yeah? What kind of internship?"

"Physical therapy." His dark eyes look so sexy in the warm glow of the room and I have to look down at the water to stop from blushing. "I'm in college to be a physical therapist."

"No shit," he says with a nod. "Smart and beautiful."

Despite how warm it already is in here, I can feel the blood rushing to my face.

Aiden clears his throat. "Sorry. That was inappropriate. I wasn't hitting on you, I was just—" His words are rushed and flimsy. He takes a deep breath and looks away. "Sorry. I know you're taken."

"Taken?" I say, holding back a sarcastic laugh. "What makes you think that?"

The look he gives me—one full of confusion—makes me feel a little weak. And giddy. It's like he's...*excited* about this new information.

"My sister told me you had a boyfriend," is all he says, but there's a hint of a question in his words.

He talked about me with his sister? Holy shit.

I shake my head. "I *did* have a boyfriend. Not anymore."

"Oh... well, I'm sorry? Or... congratulations?"

I chuckle. "I think both options are appropriate for my screwed up life."

He leans forward, keeping his casted arm resting outside of the hot tub. "Wanna talk about it?"

I'm about to say no. Because what else do you say in a situation like this? But then I realize that the truthful answer to his question would be a resounding *yes*. I do want to talk about it. I've kept this breakup a secret from my family and my friends, and unless anyone has noticed that I deleted all three years' worth of photos of Jay from my social media, then it's going to stay secret for a while.

I want to talk. I want to let it out, and the idea of telling this total stranger is appealing. He doesn't know me, and he doesn't know Jay. He can just listen.

"Sure," I say, surprising myself and apparently Aiden as well.

A small grin appears on his lips. "I'm all ears." He frowns, shaking his head. "That's such a stupid phrase. *I'm all ears?* What does that even mean? I'm some kind of ear monster?"

I laugh, and the small room echoes with the noise, which seems like such a foreign sound to me. I haven't smiled or laughed much since I walked in on Jay screwing another girl.

Aiden seems chagrined, but I'm not sure why. He holds out his good hand. "Ignore my stupidity. I'm happy to listen."

It dawns on me now. Aiden Strauss is kind of... well... a nerd. He's gorgeous and incredibly talented on a dirt bike, but when he's talking to me he seems shy. Almost dorky. I don't know how he hasn't let the fame go to his head. I've met quite a few famous motocross racers in my life and almost all of them are total cocky jackasses. They know everyone worships the ground they walk on, and they act like it.

I feel another smile tugging at my lips. It feels better than all this crying I've done lately. In fact, I'm not even holding back tears anymore.

"Well... where do I begin..."

"Start from the beginning. I've got all night." Aiden puts his good arm behind his head and leans back, resting his head in his palm. His bicep flexes, the muscles rippling down his chest. It makes a shiver run right down my spine. This guy is fitness magazine hot.

I blink to clear my mind. The beginning. Right. "Well, I've known Jay for a long time. He used to come into my dad's shop all the time and we started riding together when we were on KX80s—"

Aiden's head jerks up. "You ride?"

I nod. "I'm not very good."

"That's still pretty kick ass."

"Motocross is the greatest thing on earth," I say.

He grins like he knows exactly what I mean. I go back to my story, because now that I've started it, I feel the desperate need to finish it. I want to get it out. Maybe if I do, I'll be able to put my life with Jay out of my mind for good.

"He never really noticed me until senior year of high school. We started dating, and we've dated ever since then. Three years. Three freaking years."

My nostalgia turns into rage. "And then just a few days ago, I went to the track and I caught him hooking up with this bitch that we went to school with. She's a complete—" I exhale and shake my head. This isn't about her. It's about my shitty boyfriend. "He didn't even try to apologize. Like in the movies, you know how the guy is always like, 'wait, I can explain!' ... he didn't do that."

I look up from the bubbling water and see Aiden watching me. His jaw is set.

"I'm sorry that happened to you," he says. I can tell he means it. He looks sad, and angry. Probably a perfect mirror to what I look like, only he's vastly more good looking.

I shrug. "I'm not really sad about it anymore. I'm just pissed. I can't believe he did that, you know? I can't believe I was so stupid to not realize it was happening."

"It's not your fault," Aiden says. "Not in the slightest."

I snort. "Well if I kept him happier then—"

"No," Aiden says swiftly. "There's absolutely nothing you could have done. A cheater is a cheater. They're selfish bastards who only think about themselves. Don't even think for a second that it's your fault, because it's not."

I meet his intense gaze. "I appreciate that. I do. But you don't even know me."

"I don't have to know you to know that cheating is wrong, Jenn."

Hearing my name on his lips sends another shiver down my spine, one quite like the shiver I felt earlier when I he took off his shirt. I can't believe he remembers my name from our brief meeting at the shop. "Maybe you're right," I say.

"I am." Now there's a hint of confidence in his voice. That's the voice I expected him to have all along.

We slip into another silence. Aiden leans back, staring at the ceiling again, but I can tell he's thinking by the furrow in his brow.

"Anyway... that's my story," I say, just for something to say. "I haven't told Bella yet. I haven't told anyone. Even my parents don't know, but I'll probably tell them tonight."

"I'm sorry you were cheated on," he says, lifting his head to look at me. "You don't deserve that. If there's anything I can do, let me know."

I give him a look, and he must realize what I'm thinking— that he doesn't even know me, so what could he possibly do?

He gives me an evil grin. "I could kick his ass?"

I laugh.

"No... But thanks for offering. You don't want to break your other wrist."

He scoffs. "I said I'd kick *his* ass. I wouldn't get hurt in the process."

"Oh yeah? What if he's three hundred pounds of muscle?"

Aiden's eyes widen. "Is he?"

I can't help but smile. "No."

"Well if you need someone's ass kicked, just give me a call."

He's joking, and we're both smiling, but there's something incredibly sexy about having a guy offer to break the law for you.

"So how long are you in that cast?" I ask.

"Six weeks." He rolls his eyes as if it's the worst thing ever. "Well it started as six weeks. Now I'm down to five weeks. And then I'll finally be able to get back on the bike. I miss it so much."

"I know the feeling. I'm missing my bike but I can't bring myself to go back to the track after what happened last time."

"Does your ex ride?"

I nod.

Aiden lifts a brow. "He any good?"

His whole demeanor changes as he waits for my answer. I shake my head. "He's okay. He's not... professional or anything."

Aiden grins. "Looks like you dodged a bullet. You deserve a man who is loyal and knows how to ride a dirt bike."

I snort out a laugh. "And where am I going to find one of those?"

Aiden looks like he's about to say something, and then, after a brief second he just shrugs. "I don't know," he says softly. "But that's what you deserve."

SEVEN

Aiden

How the hell could anyone cheat on her? She's gorgeous and sweet and obviously smart. She rides dirt bikes *and* works at a bike shop. She is literally the definition of my dream girl.

And some jackhole threw her away for a fling? I don't get it. Maybe he got hit on the head and forgot he was already dating the greatest girl on this side of the planet.

I close my eyes and let the hot bubbly water soothe muscles I just worked out. It's not nearly as much fun keeping my right arm out of the water, but being in here with Jenn makes up for that small annoyance. I'm glad I took the risk and came in here. The hot tub feels amazing and I've made a new friend.

Well, maybe. I'm not sure if we're in friends territory yet. But I know that's all we can be. First of all, she's way out of my league. Like ten thousand miles away from my league. And of course, the ever-present problem that comes with being a professional motocross racer – I'll be gone as soon as this arm heals. My buddy and teammate Zach knew he couldn't get attached because of our busy schedules and yet he recently went and got himself attached anyway. Dumbass. He seems really happy though, and I guess they'll find a way to make it work. I know I wouldn't be that lucky. There's no sense in trying to date anyone.

I don't think relationship bliss is in the cards for me. The more I think about it, the more I realize I have no idea how to date someone. Motocross has been my life for as long as I can remember. Mikey and I spent every waking second at the local track, and the only time I saw girls was in school. I had a couple girlfriends in junior high, which didn't really count because all we did was hold hands in the hallway. And then in high school, I traveled every weekend for the races, going to every track within driving distance, and Mikey got famous with his professional racing deal, and I just didn't have time for girls. I like girls. A lot. But there's never been time.

Now, I'm sitting across from one of the most beautiful girls I've ever seen and she's got this content if not a little sad look on her face and I'd give my left nut to swim across the distance and kiss her.

But I wouldn't even know how.

And she's newly single, so kissing her would be a pretty jackass thing to do. She needs time to heal and get over him. And she needs to find someone better than me to date.

"So how are you liking Breaux Valley?" Jenn asks, breaking my contemplative silence.

"It's... different," I say honestly. "Quiet small towns are the complete opposite of my life back in Orlando."

She nods like she understands. "Bella said the same thing. I've never been to Orlando, but it seems fun."

"It is," I say, and then because I'm not thinking well, I add, "I'll take you some time."

She brightens. "Harry Potter world?"

"Totally," I say with a smile. "I've never been."

"What! Why not? It looks awesome."

I shrug. "I grew up in Orlando, but I don't stay there very often. Now that I'm on Team Loco I travel a lot."

"Well, we should totally go to Harry Potter world one day."

"It's a date," I say. My heart races at the words and Jenn smiles.

Her smile quickly fades and she looks sad again as she runs her fingers through the water. Her lip quivers a bit but I think she's holding back showing any emotions.

"It's okay to be sad," I tell her. "I've never been in a long relationship, but I can imagine it sucks when it's over."

She nods and her lip quivers again. She brings her wet hands to her face, wiping away tears. "I'm not sad, I'm just—" Her voice quavers and I've never wanted to hug someone as badly as I do now.

I should keep my distance. She's newly single and we're half-naked after all. I should definitely not hug her.

Jenn exhales and sits up straighter. She shakes her head as if she's clearing it of whatever she's thinking. "I'm not sad. I'm just pissed. I mean, why does he get to slip out of our relationship like that?"

She snaps her fingers but it doesn't make much noise. "He hasn't even said he's sorry, I mean what the actual hell."

Damn, she's sexy when she cusses. I like this angry side of her.

"You should make him sorry," I say.

She looks up at me, a hopeful glint in her eye. "What do you mean?"

"Get revenge."

"And how do I do that?"

I consider it for a moment. "Date his best friend. No—date his enemy! Who does he think is his biggest competition on the track? Who is faster than he is? You should date that guy."

She rolls her eyes. "That's Rafael. I really don't think I

should date a thirty-year-old husband and father."

"Damn," I say, shaking my head. "Yeah, probably shouldn't do that."

She grins. "Plus he works at my dad's shop and he's kind of like a brother to me, so that would just be terrible."

I laugh. "Okay, so don't date the faster racer. Date someone he doesn't like."

She lets her fingers float on the bubbly surface of the water. I'm trying to be a good friend here but I'd be lying if I said I wasn't wishing I could see that bikini under all these bubbles.

"Jay has a lot of enemies," she says finally. "He's kind of an asshole. But I can't exactly snap my fingers and date some guy."

Something tells me she could do just that if she had the desire.

"Maybe I should just go on with my life and act like it didn't affect me," she says, running her fingers through the water. "I'll keep going to the track and riding and he can just piss off. I'll ignore him. I'll show that I'm living my life just fine without him."

A delightful and terrible idea comes to me. "Or... you could get a fake boyfriend."

"What, like hire an escort?" she says with a snort.

I shake my head. "Date a professional racer."

Her eyes go wide. I swear I think she might blush. Her tongue slips across her bottom lip before she speaks. "And that professional racer would be..."

I grin and point to myself. "Aiden Strauss, five week fake lover, at your service."

She laughs. Actually laughs. Her eyes crinkle at the corners and the sound of her happiness is like music to my ears.

She shakes her head and flicks her fingers in the water, sending a small bit of it at my chest. "Very funny," she says.

"Hey! I'm being serious." I put a hand to my chest like I'm

offended. "Am I not good enough? I know I'm broken, but I am still a pro. I bet it would piss the hell out of your ex."

"It's more like you're *too* good," she says, her eyes meeting mine for just a fraction of a second before darting away. "You're famous. No one would believe you'd actually date me."

This girl is so very wrong. I would date her in a heartbeat if I thought I could. If I lived here full time and didn't have a crazy career, I'd be putting all the moves on her, trying to make her mine.

Instead, I play it cool. "It's easy. Picture it—you arrive at the track with Aiden Strauss. Everyone's like *'oh my god, there's a famous racer!'* and as they approach me for an autograph, I slide my arm around you and tug you close to me. I place a kiss on your head. All the girls swoon and wish they were you."

Her mouth parts slightly as she watches me talk. I take her interest as encouragement to keep talking out this fantasy. "I say, 'no autographs right now.. I'm with my girl' and everyone looks sad but they're also looking at you with admiration. I mean, you're dating THE Aiden Strauss. We sit on the bleachers and watch the races, and I snuggle you close to my side, keeping my arm possessively around you. If you're thirsty, I get you a drink. I am a doting, loyal, caring boyfriend. That jackhole ex of yours shows up and someone says, 'dude did you see Jenn's new boyfriend?' and he looks over and sees you being perfectly happy with a *real* man, and he suddenly realizes his mistake. His dick shrivels up and falls off because it knows he will never be man enough to date again."

Jenn bursts out laughing. "Oh my God," she says, covering her mouth with her hand. "That was perfect."

"I know. I should be a romance author or something."

When her laughter subsides, she bites down on her bottom lip, looking a little shy. Like maybe she wants to accept my offer but doesn't know how.

"What have you got to lose?" I say. "Five week fake boyfriend. I guarantee you it'll piss him off. You'll get your revenge."

She shakes her head. "I can't use you like that."

"It's not using me," I say. "I'm offering. I'm stuck here for the next five weeks so what else would I be doing? Plus, you can even dump me when it's over."

"Aww, I wouldn't dump you," she says playfully. It sends some kind of shockwave right through my heart. I know she's playing, but I like hearing the words.

"This is silly," she says after a beat. "I mean… pretend dating? You're not really serious, are you?"

"I'm dead serious," I say. "It'd be an honor to be your fake boyfriend."

In my head, I substitute the word fake for real, and it makes my insides go all fuzzy. God, I would love to be her real boyfriend. I'd love a life that allows relationships. Of course, who knows if I'd be any good at it. Maybe this fake thing is exactly what I need. I can figure out exactly how to be a good boyfriend for when the time comes that I can date without my career getting in the way.

I look across at Jenn and I know I'm shooting myself in the foot. There's no way I won't fall for her just a little bit, even though I know it's all pretend. She's the whole package. But it's better this way. We can go into it knowing it's just a fling, just a pretend arrangement. That way no one gets hurt.

It's probably better if she turns me down, but I desperately hope she says yes.

"So what'll it be?" I ask, my heart pounding. "Want to fake date me and piss off your ex?"

Her beautiful pink lips slide into a grin. Her eyes narrow. "I think you're crazy. But… maybe I'm crazy too."

I smirk. "So let's be crazy together."

EIGHT

Jenn

I am nervous all morning at work. It's Saturday and it's a race day at the local track. Race days are crazy busy, but that's not why it feels like there's a rock lodged in my throat and butterflies doing acrobatics in my stomach.

Jay hasn't come in yet.

Thirty Six Cycles sells a premium racing gas that we have to import from some fuel company and it's very expensive. All the fastest riders stop by our shop before race days to buy a few gallons of it. Jay always stops by first thing in the morning on race days.

It's two hours until the races begin, and he hasn't come in yet. I stand anxiously behind the counter, my eyes darting to the door every time someone comes in. I'm still not ready to see him. I don't want to talk to him. I don't want to look at him and remember how he looked the last time I saw him.

Last night I broke the news to my parents. I took the easy way out told them over a text message. I was feeling giddy and stupid after spending an hour in the hot tub with Aiden freaking Strauss, and he had almost convinced me that it would be fun to be his pretend girlfriend. As soon as I got home, I sent my parents a text through our family group chat that said:

I BROKE UP WITH *J*AY. *I don't want to talk about it. It's really not a big deal, I just wanted you to know.*

MOM HAD CALLED me immediately after, and I did my best fake happy voice, acting like nothing was wrong and that it was totally fine. I didn't tell them that he cheated. Not to save his integrity or anything but, honestly because I worry my dad would try to kick his ass or something.

Now, my news is out in the open, and I'm at work and my dad is acting normal toward me, which is great. I know my parents assumed Jay and I would probably get married one day, and of course I assumed that too.

Oh well. It's not happening. Time to move on.

The door to the shop opens and I flinch. But it's not him, thank God. It's just the dad of a kid who races every weekend. I smile and greet him and sell him some race gas and then let out a long sigh of relief.

I check my watch again. Jay is always at the races by now. He's probably not coming. He should know better than to show up here now.

Of course, there's no other place within a hundred miles to buy race gas, so who knows. We live in a small town and I know I'll see him again at some point, but I'm going to cherish every moment I have until that happens.

I feel a buzz in the back pocket of my shorts and I take out my phone. I'm still not used to the new background photo – a cute cat picture I found online – but the name on my screen is very familiar.

. . .

JAY: *you ready to talk yet?*

I STARE, open-mouthed at the text message. What is his deal? Am I ready to talk? Of course I don't want to talk! I don't owe him a talk. I don't owe him *shit*.

I put the phone back in my pocket, leaving his pathetic text unanswered.

When the shop door opens again, my heart leaps into overdrive. Jay's text was about ten minutes ago and that's about how long it would take him to drive here from his house. Oh God. *Please* don't be him. The store is filled with customers and I can't stand the idea of facing my cheating ex when I'm at work.

A familiar figure walks inside, setting my fears at ease. But just as quickly as I'm relieved that it's not Jay, I get nervous again.

Because it's Aiden.

He looks incredibly sexy in a pair of black shorts, Adidas shoes, and a blue Team Loco shirt that fits him like it was designed for his muscular body. Hell, maybe it was. It looks like a plain T-shirt from here, but it can't possibly be plain because he makes it look so good.

He lifts the sunglasses off his eyes and grins at me from across the shop. His dark hair is a little messy but in this sexy way, like it's just waiting for me to run my hands through it. To grip my hand in his hair and tug his mouth to mine...

"Morning," he says, walking up to the counter. His lips tip up in this smirk that makes my stomach tense up. He leans his elbows on the counter in front of me. "I figured I would find you here. We made a huge mistake last night."

My throat goes dry. I should have seen this coming. Of

course he doesn't want to pretend to be anything with me. God, I feel like an idiot.

"Yeah, sorry—" I begin, but he cuts me off by sliding his phone across the counter.

"We forgot to exchange numbers."

I stare at him as I realize he was just making a stupid joke earlier. He grins at me.

"Don't look so scared, it's just a number."

I snap out of it real quick. "I'm not scared," I say sarcastically as I take his phone. The screen is already unlocked. With shaking fingers, I type in my number and save it. I can't believe I'm this nervous to be this close to a guy.

"Thanks babe," he says, sliding his phone back into his pocket. He holds out his good hand toward me. "Your turn."

I take out my phone, unlock the screen and immediately close out my texts that were still open. I go to the contacts list and create a new one, then hand him my phone.

He's a little clumsy using a phone with only his left hand, and he brings his cast up to steady it. I watch him, how his bottom lip turns under his teeth while he types in his number. God, everything this guy does is sexy. I wonder if being that good looking is some kind of supernatural skill that makes him faster on a dirt bike.

Instead of handing my phone back, he presses the home screen button. He frowns. "Well, that's not going to do," he says, looking up at me.

"What's not going to do?" I ask.

He glances around then gives me a mischievous look. "Can I come back there or is there some no customers allowed behind the counter rule?"

"Technically, that's a rule I guess, but you're not a customer. You're Aiden Strauss and I'm sure my dad would let you do anything you want."

"Even date his daughter?" he says, his eyebrows lifting.

I blush a furious shade of red. I hadn't even thought about that when we talked last night. If I'm going to pretend date Aiden, my family would find out. Should I tell them the truth, that it's a lie?

Aiden walks behind the counter, rules be damned, and holds up my phone. "Time for a new background photo," he says.

With the camera on, he holds it out and wraps his casted arm around me. I smile like we're taking a selfie, but at the last second, Aiden presses a kiss to my cheek. *Snap.*

He lets go of me and I feel the sudden urge to press myself against his body again, but I'm sane enough to hold back. He grins and hands me my phone.

"There you go. Perfect background photo."

I look down at the screen. He's already set it as my wallpaper. We look good. Happy. We look like a real couple.

"Text it to me?" Aiden asks as he walks back around the counter to the customer side. "I need a new background, too."

While I'm texting him the photo, my dad pops out from the back of the shop, and calls out Aiden's name.

"Good to see you!" Dad says, clapping him on the back. "What can I help you with today?"

"Oh, I'm just here to see Jenn," Aiden says. My dad's smile widens. Whatever I thought my dad's reaction would be, this isn't it. "Well, here she is," he says, motioning to me. "You take good care of my boy," Dad tells me before walking off to join another customer.

"That's Aiden Strauss over there!" Dad tells the customer, his voice booming with pride as if Aiden were his own son.

"Your dad's cool," Aiden tells me.

I roll my eyes. "He's starstruck."

A little boy runs up to Aiden and taps his arm. "Mr.

Strauss?" he says in a tiny voice. When Aiden turns to him, he holds out a crayon and a coloring book. "Can I have your autograph?"

"Sure you can, little buddy." Aiden kneels down and takes the crayon, holding it awkwardly in his casted hand.

The coloring book is dirt bike themed, and Aiden turns to a fresh page that features a cartoon guy on a dirt bike. He signs it real big.

A few feet away, I see the boy's mother watching him with a smile on her face. "Tell him thank you," she whispers to her son.

"Thank you!" the boy practically yells as Aiden hands back the autograph.

"You're quite welcome," Aiden says.

He's so cute when he's talking to kids. His voice gets softer and sweeter.

Over the next half an hour, all the customers want to talk to him, and he seems happy to talk back. He signs autographs and poses for photos, and gives some riding advice to a few teenagers I recognize from the track.

After a while, everyone clears out because the races are about to start. I pretend to be busy on the store's computer while my dad talks with Aiden a bit. But once Rafael calls Dad back into the shop with a question, we are once again alone.

"The celebrity of Breaux Valley," I say, tossing a wadded up post-it note to Aiden.

He catches it in his left hand. "I like people," he says. "I really like them when they're not asking about my brother."

"Your brother?" I say without thinking. Then I remember. Mikey Strauss—the famous motocross racer who came on the scene a few years before Aiden did. He was arrested for drugs and I haven't seen him again. It was a pretty big scandal in the professional motocross world.

I shrug. "You're not your brother."

"That's for damn sure," Aiden says, running his finger over a sticker on the counter. "He had all the natural talent. I've had to work my ass off to go pro. He just slid into it like the entire sport of motocross was made for him."

"Does he still ride?" I ask, choosing my words carefully because I can tell this is a sensitive topic for Aiden.

He shakes his head. "Every day I'm worried he might start back, but he's too out of shape and lazy these days. Jail kind of ruined him. Actually—it was probably the drugs."

I don't know what to say, so I just nod quietly.

"Anyway," Aiden says, smacking his good hand flat on the counter. "I'm here to take you on a date."

"A date?" I say with a snort. "I'm at work."

"So after work."

I hesitate, trying to figure out if this is joke. "I have a ton of homework to do."

Aiden is undeterred. "So tomorrow then. Sunday."

"Why are we going on a date?" I ask.

"Because we're *fake dating*," he says, whispering the last two words. "You can't pretend to date someone without going on dates."

I tuck my hair behind my ears. "I didn't think we were actually doing that."

"Of course we are," he says. "Until that jackass ex of yours realizes the mistake he made." He reaches across the counter and puts his hand on top of mine. "So, girlfriend, are you free tomorrow for a pretend date that's going to blow your mind?"

I laugh. "If it's pretend, we could just pretend we went on a date and not actually do it."

"No way. This is a small town, babe. We need to be seen in public. You can't just call up your ex and tell him you found someone new—it doesn't work that way. You have to be out in public. Have someone else see you and tell him. Trust me, he'll hate finding out that way. He has to find out from the grapevine that the best girl he ever dated has moved on to someone better."

The look he gives me sends a shiver right up my spine. God, he's gorgeous. I would give anything to have him ask me on a real date. But I guess this is all I get. Better strike while the iron is hot and all that.

"Okay," I say. "Sunday it is."

He grins. "I'll pick you up around noon. Wear clothes like you have on now."

I look down. "Shorts and a Thirty Six Cycles shirt?"

He grins. "Yeah. No high heels or anything fancy. I'm taking you on a fun date."

"I'm intrigued," I say.

He taps his fingers on the countertop. "Oh, and I'll be picking you up in my sister's car. Which is actually your old car."

I laugh. I love that Aiden is fun and laid back. I love that he doesn't get all alpha male and refuse to drive a black Camaro that belongs to his sister. Jay hated my car. He would never drive it and he hated when I wanted to drive us somewhere. He had to be in his massive monster truck and he had to be in charge, always.

I never realized it back then, but now I do. A guy who is comfortable driving his little sister's car is a much sexier trait than any positive thing I ever saw in Jay's personality.

NINE

Aiden

Bella pokes her head into the guest room that's temporarily my room at Grandma's house. She watches me while I stare into the mirror, attempting to fix my hair that's always messy. It's like I've got permanent helmet hair from pulling the thing on and off my head so many years of my life.

Besides my jacked up hair, I think I look good. The red cast isn't exactly a trendy fashion accessory, but there's nothing I can do about that. I slip on my shoes and take one last look at myself in the mirror.

"So where exactly are you taking my car?" Bella asks. "You look way too excited to be going somewhere boring."

Last night, when I asked to borrow her car today, she agreed without so much as a second thought. Now she's watching me with narrowed eyes like she thinks I'm trying to pull one over on her.

Well, I guess I kind of am. I decide not to lie to my little sister.

"I'm taking Jenn somewhere fun for the day."

Her jaw drops. "Jenn? Aiden, she has a boyfriend!"

I shake my head. "Not anymore. The bastard cheated on her."

"What!" My sister's eyes widen. "How do you know this and I don't?"

I shrug and get my wallet off the nightstand. "I ran into her at the gym and she told me. And now we have a plan to get revenge on the asshole."

Bella walks inside my room, hands on her hips. She looks slightly intimidating even though she's so much shorter than I am. "What does that mean? You can't just steal her when she just broke up! You'll only hurt her again."

"No, it's not like that, Bells. I promise. She wanted to get even with him for cheating on her, so we're pretending that we're dating. It's just to piss him off."

Bella seems to consider it for a moment, but she doesn't take her hands off her hips. "If you're *pretending* to date, why are you going out together today?"

I tap my phone on top of her head before I put it in my pocket. "To keep up appearances," I say.

She sighs and follows me out into the hallway. "She's my friend, Aiden. Don't hurt her."

I turn to my sister, giving her a sincere look. I wish I could tell her that I'm the only one in danger of getting hurt here, but I'm not about to reveal *that* embarrassing detail. I put my hands on her shoulders and smile. "You don't have to worry. We're friends. We're just messing with her ex. The plan is that she'll dump me in a few weeks before I go back to racing and she'll look like the badass who dumped Aiden Strauss."

Bella rolls her eyes. "That's a stupid plan."

I grin and take her car keys off the hook near the door. I can't say I disagree with my sister—it is a stupid plan—but people do stupid things when it means they get to spend time with a beautiful girl.

I FOLLOW the GPS on my phone as it leads me a few miles across town to the address Jenn gave me. The house looks like a two story garage, with a garage on bottom and a house up top. There's a matching brick home on the other side of the yard that's much bigger than this one. I'm guessing her parents live there. I'm glad this small garage house has its own driveway, because if Mr. Doherty saw me drive up at his house, he'd probably rush out here and beg me to hang out with him all day.

I'm weirdly nervous as I get out of the car and walk up the outside steps to the second floor. I'm trying to think about the last time I had a date. Have I *ever* had a date?

I remember this time in eighth grade when Mikey drove me and Amber Sosa to the mall where we walked around holding hands for two hours until we had to be back home. I guess that was a date. Then there was a couple of motocross girls who followed me around the race track and kissed me in the bed of Mikey's truck. I never really took those girls on dates. They just showed up every weekend at the races and acted like my girlfriend. I lost my virginity in the back seat of my first truck when I was eighteen—not because I was in a loving relationship but because Leah Brant and I had been flirting all weekend and got drunk off a bottle of Jack Daniels that I found in Mikey's ice chest.

Damn. I'm seriously out of practice.

And I have not had an amazing dating life.

I swallow my nerves and knock on the door. Jenn opens it, smiling at me in this way that washes away my nerves. Her hair is tied into a bun at the top of her head, with little wispy strands hanging in front of her face. It's cute as hell.

"How do I look?" she says, taking a step back and motioning to her clothing. "Is this casual enough for the day's activities?"

She's wearing black shorts that show off her tanned legs and a white V-neck shirt with a black beaded necklace.

I say the first word that comes to mind. "Beautiful."

She laughs like I'm being silly and slings her purse over her shoulder. I'm still standing outside at the top of the stairs, but the scent of sugary sweetness, like cupcakes, flows out of her living room. It smells just like the car does, and it's a good smell.

"Ready to go?" she asks.

I nod and step out of the way so she can come outside and lock her door. The whole walk back to my car I'm wrestling with wondering if I should open her door for her or not. If this were a real date, then yeah, I would. But it's technically just a fake date and no one is around right now to see us so—

Screw it, I open the door.

She slides into the passenger seat of her old car, looks up at me and grins. "Thanks."

Looks like I made the right decision.

I don't use the GPS because I want our destination to be a secret, so instead, I ask Jenn to give me directions to the main road. I've memorized how to get there once we get off the back roads.

"So what's been up?" I ask, not wanting to look over at her because I'm afraid I'll get caught up in staring into her gorgeous eyes and won't be able to drive safely.

"School," she says, blowing a raspberry with her lips. "So much school work."

"Oh? Like what kind of work?"

Normally I'm a regular guy. I can talk and hang out and make small chit chat with anyone. Half of my job requires talking to fans and interviewers and my teammates. Yet as we drive, our bodies so close together in this car that smells like her, and I listen to her sweet voice talking, I feel like a little kid with a crush so big it's suffocating me.

Since I don't trust myself to talk, I just ask questions and let her talk about her college work. Soon, I see the exit sign and I pull off the road.

"Hmm," Jenn says, watching the road. "I still have no idea where we're going."

I grin. "You'll see in about two minutes."

She looks over at me, her eyes wide and eager. "This is exciting. Jay never took me on surprise dates."

I don't know why but my heart really warms up at that.

There's no hiding where we're going once I turn into the parking lot. The building takes up the entire space, like it was made out of an old Wal-Mart or something.

"Whaaat!" Jenn says, her mouth opening wide as she peers up at the JACK'S TRAMPOLINE PARK sign. "No way!"

I park and look over at her. "Have you been here before?"

She shakes her head. "No, but it looks awesome."

"Let's go see for ourselves," I say.

I'd spent no less than three hours Googling all over Louisiana last night, trying to think of a great place to take Jenn on a first fake date. The movies are lame, and getting dinner is lame. Plus, she's newly heartbroken and stressed with school and work, so I thought we should do something fun. Who cares if we're in our twenties and not exactly kids anymore? Even the website said adults were allowed.

We step into the trampoline park and I'm sure my eyes are as wide and excited as Jenn's. The building is huge. The walls are painted in bright colors, and just beyond the registration desk, the entire flooring turns to trampolines. There are trampoline dodgeball courts, and freestyle courts with angled trampolines on the walls, a ball pit and a foam pit with really high ledges you can jump off.

To the left is the party room and an unlimited pizza buffet. To the right is an arcade room. This place has everything.

Jenn grabs my hand and squeezes it. "This looks awesome!"

The smile on her face tells me I picked the perfect place. I pay for both of us to have an unlimited all day pass, shooing Jenn away when she tries to pay for herself.

"This is a date," I tell her. "My treat."

She rolls her eyes but thanks me anyway.

We leave our shoes and the contents of our pockets in a locker and put on these big fluffy socks they give you that's supposed to make the trampolines more fun.

"I'm surprised they let you in here with that broken arm," Jenn says as she stands up, admiring the way the socks swallow up her feet.

"Did you see all those liability waivers we signed?" I say with a laugh. "I don't think they care."

"Where to first?" Jenn says, peering out at the trampoline park. The dodgeball area has a serious game going with two dozen kids, and I know we're not about to join them. They'd slaughter us.

"Let's jump our way to the ball pit," I say, throwing her a cocky grin. "First one there wins."

We take off running, up the stairs to the trampoline floors, and then we both slow down. Turns out it's hard to run on lots of trampolines.

Jenn laughs and starts jumping on one, and our competition is forgotten. We bounce around and race each other from one end to the other. When I get to the end of the line, I turn and bounce my back off the trampoline against the vertical wall. After two tries, I start to get cocky and I bounce into it and do a backflip.

When I emerge, hands in the air and victorious, Jenn is

standing on a nearby trampoline watching me with this look that makes my insides melt.

"That was ... cool," she says. Her cheeks are flushed, and I want to think she's blushing over me, but it's probably just because we're running around acting like maniacs.

We play around for another hour, and I can see Jenn's stress melting away with each jump. I think my stresses are disappearing too, and I hadn't realized I had so many things that were bothering me. Missing motocross sucks. It's the only thing in my life, and my main stress. But there's something else too, some hidden pain lurking just under the surface and jumping around with Jenn is making me realize what it is.

Loneliness. I've spent so many months being alone. Working out, riding, racing, traveling. Sure, the guys are with me a lot, but it's not like you talk about serious things with the guys. I hadn't known my sister moved out. I don't even know what hairstyle my mom has right now—not that I care to know—but I never see my family anymore. I didn't want anyone or anything in my life until recently.

I don't want this day to ever end.

Once we're exhausted and starving, Jenn and I head to the food court and get pizza. My legs feel like jelly, but in a good way. I didn't realize how much of a workout it would be to jump on trampolines for hours. I could probably skip the gym tonight. Maybe if Jenn wants to hang out after this, I'll have an even better excuse to skip the gym.

We play some arcade games after lunch because the signs all over the walls suggest that you wait half an hour after eating to get back to jumping.

Jenn plays a particularly epic game of air hockey, beating me 7 to 3, and then she sets the puck down and smiles at me. "There's something I want to do before we leave," she says.

"What's that?"

She turns to the trampoline park and points toward the far corner.

"The ball pit?" I say.

Her eyes turn mischievous. "I want to jump off the ledge."

I grin. "Let's do it."

The ledge is a foam staircase that takes you about twenty feet in the air and you can jump off it into a massive ball pit. It's unlike any ball pit I've ever seen. The balls are made of foam instead of plastic, and it's about six feet deep. I grab Jenn's hand and walk us across the trampoline floor and over to the foam steps of the ledge.

We climb up it, which is also a work out because foam steps are squishy and difficult, but finally we make it to the top. There's no one in the ball pit right now, so it feels like we have this little corner of the world to ourselves.

"Wanna go first?" I ask as we walk up to the ledge.

Jenn stares down it, biting her lip. "Okay, now I'm scared."

"It's not far," I say. "You'll be in the balls before you know it."

She gives me a look. "That's what she said?"

I laugh. "Yeah, bad wording on my part."

Jenn takes my hand and we stand right at the edge, our toes hanging over. She takes a deep breath, then closes her eyes. "I can't look. Just tell me when to jump and we'll do it together."

"You sure?"

She nods eagerly, her eyes still squeezed shut.

"Okay... three... two..."

I leap forward and pull her with me, using my good hand to wrap around her waist as we fall. She squeals in delight as we tumble down, and I land on my back on the foam balls, Jenn squeezed on top of me.

"Oh my god!" she says, opening her eyes. "That was so much fun!"

I'm out of breath, and in a little pain. I'd held my cast out and away from us, but the impact still jarred it a little. Jenn is still lying on top of me, and my good arm is still around her back. Her boobs are pressed against my chest and her sugary smell is making me all kinds of turned on.

Right after impact, the balls start to sag. "Are we sinking?" she says, looking around.

"Looks like it," I breathe, but I'm not looking at the balls. I'm looking at her.

We sink a little further, and now we're half covered in foam. Jenn is making no move to climb off me, and I'm making no move to let her go.

She gazes into my eyes, and in that moment, I just know. She wants it as badly as I do. I slide my good hand up her back and run my fingers through her hair.

Then I close my eyes and kiss her.

To my great relief, she kisses me back. Her lips are salty and sweet and soft as hell. I can feel our bodies rocking slightly to the heaving pounding of our hearts. I'm not sure if it's from the adrenaline of falling or from being this close together. We sink deeper into the ball pit and I deepen the kiss, parting her lips with mine. I realize I am inexperienced in kissing—unpracticed —but we find our way together. She grabs my face with her hands and kisses me back like she means it. Like she's been waiting all day to do just this.

And it occurs to me now, fake relationship or not, that we might have a lot more in common than we think.

TEN

Jenn

Physiology is the most boring class I'm taking this semester. It's boring on a normal day, but it's nearly unbearable today. Today is definitely not normal.

Because two days ago, Aiden kissed me.

As my professor drones on with his boring lecture about cell membrane function, I can't help but let my mind wander back to that ball pit. I'd felt Aiden's muscular body pressed underneath mine. His arm was warm, protective, as it wrapped around me. His lips were soft and timid at first, like kissing me was something he wanted to make sure he got right. For those few minutes, I was lost in Aiden's embrace, my thoughts and worries and stress just washed away with a kiss.

And then eventually, we had to get back to reality. Which is why I'm currently sitting in my class at the university instead of staying in that ball pit snuggled up with Aiden for eternity.

I draw in a slow breath and let it out in a sigh. This is bad. I'm not supposed to be moving through my life like a lovestruck zombie who can't wait to see Aiden again. This is all fake. I knew it going into it, and I know it now. Fake, fake, fake.

I look up and realize the professor has changed slides on the overhead projector. Shit. I scramble to type it all on my laptop before he switches slides again. I don't even know what he's talking about now. This class is important, and I need to pay attention.

I make myself sit up straighter, hoping that a good posture will somehow erase daydreams of kissing Aiden from my mind. It does not work. I glance around the class and see the other students, most of them looking bored, but still paying attention. Am I the only one here who can't focus?

Yesterday was another long work day. I spent eight hours at the shop with my dad and then went to LaValle for my internship. Martha, my director, let me schedule part-time evening hours as an intern so I can keep working at the shop. I'm not exactly broke, but I definitely need my meager paycheck each week to keep my bills paid. I don't have to pay rent, but I do have to pay my truck note, utility bills, and everything else.

Because of my busy schedule, I hadn't seen Aiden yesterday, but I guess I shouldn't have expected to see him. After the trampoline park, we said we'd have another fake date "soon" but neither of us clarified what soon meant. Like an idiot, I'd kept my phone close by yesterday just in case Aiden wanted to text me.

He didn't.

And that's totally cool. This is a fake relationship after all.

Dammit, Jenn. I take another deep breath. I tell myself, yet again, to stop thinking about this guy. Like, seriously. Just stop it. He's fake. He's a famous racer and he's doing me a favor to get back at Jay, and none of it is real and he'll be gone in a few weeks anyway.

I spend the rest of the class period diligently taking notes and repeating everything the professor says in my head. That way, there's no room for stupid thoughts about a guy to bother me.

After the lecture is over, I scoop up my laptop and textbook and make my way out into the courtyard. There's some pop-up food truck in the parking lot selling tacos for charity. It looks pretty good, but the line is ridiculously long. Part of me wants to stay, join the long line and make small talk with the other people there. It could be fun, breaking out of my shell. Expanding my friends circle to include new people and not just the same people I've known my whole life from my tiny town and from motocross.

Seriously, every single friend I have is also friends with Jay. Every person I know knows me as Jay's longtime girlfriend. And every time I run into someone at the shop or in the grocery store, they ask about him. Sometimes I just wish I had a different set of friends, people who know me as me. Not as some prick's girlfriend.

Despite my desperate need for new friends, my anxiety gets the best of me and I walk right past the taco truck and toward the parking lot. I'll make new friends some other day.

I'm staring at my text messages with Aiden while I walk, wondering if there's something I could text him that would be fun and cute and not make me look desperate to talk to him again. But really, there's nothing. We have no reason to talk because we're not really dating. I don't even think we're really friends. We're just two people pulling off a scheme together.

With a sigh, I put my phone away, deciding not to text him. I don't want to look pathetic or desperate.

"Hey there," a familiar voice says.

At first I think maybe he's not talking to me, but then I see him standing there, leaning against my truck like he's been waiting here a while.

I swallow. It's too late to turn around.

He's seen me and I've seen him.

I curse under my breath, and hold out my keys, pressing the

unlock button. "You're in my way," I say, stopping several feet in front of him.

Jay puts on a smile like he thinks that's going to fix everything.

"Let's talk."

"There's nothing to talk about, except that you're standing in front of my door, so please move."

"Jenn, don't be stubborn."

I grit my teeth. I hate being called stubborn.

Jay stands there, four inches taller than me and much wider. He's not as tall as Aiden, I think, but then those thoughts are scared away when Jay tilts his head and holds out his arms like he wants a hug.

A hug? Yeah not happening.

I cross my arms over my chest, as if to make it very obvious they won't be wrapping around him any time soon. "I'm not hugging you. Get out of my way."

"No need to be rude," he says.

"Leave me alone," I say. My backpack is slung over my shoulder, getting heavier by the second with the weight of my books and laptop. I'm still holding my keys, and I could maybe press the panic button but I doubt that would do much to scare him off. There's nothing I can do right now.

I exhale through my nose, keeping my jaw clenched. "What do you want?"

He brightens, a half smile quirking on his lips. He knows he's won this round and I hate him for it. "I just want to talk, baby."

I shake my head. "I'm not your baby."

"Yes you are, Jenn. You know you are. You're my soul mate, and I love you." His eyes focus on me. "And I know you love me."

I shake my head again. "Not anymore."

He snorts. "Yes, you do. Love doesn't just go away. Look, I gave you a little break, but now it's time to get things back the way they were."

"A break?" I say, my voice getting louder. "You gave me a break *up*."

He actually has the gall to look offended. "Jenn, baby, we did not break up."

"Yes, we did. We were broken up the second you slept with Miranda."

He rolls his eyes and it's the same look he makes when I'm telling a customer what type of oil they should use, or what brand of bike is better, and he thinks I'm an idiot and that he knows better than I do.

"Baby, that was a one time mistake. You know that."

"All I know is that you cheated on me," I say, gritting my teeth. "I don't need to know anything else."

"Baby... you need to calm down. You've got it all wrong. I don't even like that girl. I like you. I *love* you."

He takes a step toward me and I take one step back. "Baby, don't be like this."

I hate the way he's looking at me right now. It's like he thinks I'll just suck it up and forgive him. "Why did you do it?" I ask. I hate myself for caring, but deep down I want to know. I want to know what's so bad about me that would make my boyfriend of three years cheat on me with someone else.

He shrugs. "Hell, I don't know."

I give him a look. "Seriously? You ruined our relationship and you don't even know why?"

"Baby, I was just horny. That's how guys are. She was all up on me and I couldn't say no. I wanted to, but you know I can't. That's just how guys are. We can't help it."

"That is not a good enough answer."

Jay throws his hands up in the air. "I don't know what else

you want from me, Jenn. That's the damn truth. *She* came on to me. I didn't ask for it. She caught me in a bad moment and got naked, and what was I supposed to do?"

"Um, tell her to leave?" I say, sarcasm heavy in my voice. "That's what you do. You stay away from track whores and stay faithful to your girlfriend."

"I am faithful," he says, putting a hand to his chest. "I stay faithful to you. I only love you. I only want you. Miranda was just sex. But with you, it's love."

He takes another step forward, and now he's no longer blocking the driver's side door of my truck. I must stare at it too long, because suddenly he backs up, pressing his body to the tuck again.

"You're not leaving, Jenn. Not until we talk this out."

Dammit.

"Did you even think about me?" I ask, my voice cracking. "When you were with her, did I ever cross your mind? Did you think for one second that it might be wrong?"

"Hell no," he says so quickly that I can tell he's not lying. "Babe I'm never thinking of you during that."

My breath catches. "Never?"

He shakes his head. "Not once."

My whole body goes cold. He's just admitted to cheating on me more than one time. "And how many times have you cheated on me?"

"It's not cheating. It's just sex. Seriously. Don't be so uptight. If you had bothered to knock, then you wouldn't have even had to see it."

White hot rage burns from my heart down to my toes. What a bastard. I keep my face expressionless. I know if I keep talking then he'll keep blocking my door. All I want to do is go home and maybe cry. I don't know what I'm feeling right now, besides pure unbidden rage. I can't believe I was so stupid.

I know he won't leave. Not if I ask nicely. So I decide to trick him.

"There's a taco truck across campus," I say, my voice steady. I don't let my emotions show. "Let's get lunch and we can talk."

He smiles. "Good. Let's go."

I sling my backpack off my shoulder. "Let me put my backpack up first," I say.

Just like I'd hoped, he steps away. My heart pounds as I open my truck door. I lean in to drop my backpack on the seat, and then with a quick glance backward, I see Jay checking his cell phone. I jump up into the truck and close the door behind me. His head snaps up, eyes wide. He lunges for me I press the door lock button just before he grabs the handle. His nostrils flare.

I grin and start my engine.

"What the hell, Jenn?" Jay yells through the closed window.

I press my middle finger to the glass and drive off.

ELEVEN

Aiden

My legs are screaming from the workout I did this morning. I probably overdid it, but I was desperate to do something to stay fit. I've learned that I can't exactly run because it jostles my wrist too much and I'll be in severe pain the next day, so instead I'd hit the stationary bike and pedaled for three straight hours this morning. And while the bike worked at making me exhausted and starving, it did not stop me from thinking about Jenn. I've been going to the gym every morning instead of afternoons, which is when I'm pretty sure she works. I'm not trying to avoid her, I'm just trying to save my sanity. I don't want to become that creepy stalker guy.

She hasn't texted me in a few days and now we're stuck in that mind game of text uncertainty. Should I text her? Does she want me to? Or has she forgotten about me? I don't want to seem too clingy or annoying. I'd thought real-life dating was stressful, but fake dating is just as bad. Especially when you're actually crushing on your fake girlfriend.

That day at the trampoline park keeps running through my mind, and I analyze it wondering if there's something I missed the last million times I thought about it. Like maybe I'd missed some small hint that means she didn't like being with me. But there's nothing. We'd had a blast. It was the most fun I've had in a very long time. It was the best kiss I've had in well—ever.

Now I just don't know if I should reach out to her or not. So I'm sitting here on Grandma's couch, lazily watching some reality TV show about people who build extravagant dog houses. My sister does her homeschooling in the morning, so I wait around, bored and thinking about Jenn, until Bella finally leaves her room.

"All done with school work?" I ask.

She nods. "It only takes a few hours and it's so much better than regular school where I'd be stuck there all day." She's still wearing her pajamas, and I can't say I blame her for preferring homeschool. It sounds awesome. She sits next to me on the couch.

"I love this show," she says. "Last time they made dog houses for celebrities."

"I'm bored, Bells. What is there to do?"

She perks up. "Actually... there is something going on tonight but I don't know if you'd like it."

I turn to her. "I'm so bored I'd be down for pretty much anything."

My sister grins. "What about funnel cakes?"

My lip curls. "Oh, God, no." With that one sentence, she made me remember the time she and I had a funnel cake eating contest in Miami and we both ate so much we puked. I can't stand the thought of funnel cakes now. Bella laughs her evil little sister laugh. "The fall festival is this week. There's carnival rides and food and stuff. I'm going to meet some of my friends there, but you can come if you want. We could stay far away from the funnel cakes."

"Which friends?" I ask.

She narrows her eyes at me. "My teenager friends. But I guess I could invite Jenn if you wanted…"

"Am I that obvious?" I say with a snort.

Bella rolls her eyes. "You never did tell me how your fake date went," she says, making air quotes over the word date.

I shrug. "It was fun. I think she had a good time."

"And did you have a good time?"

"Of course." I'm still picturing the awkward way I dropped her back off at her house, where I think we both wanted to kiss goodbye but knew we shouldn't. I wish I had gone for it.

Bella throws a couch pillow at me. "You like her!"

I shake my head, and even throw in an annoyed sigh like I'm just too casual to be bothered with her teasing. I hope she buys it. "It's just for fun," I say. "We're making people *think* we're dating."

"Well, no better place than to take her to the fall festival," Bella says.

"I'll ask her," I say, leaning forward to get my phone off the coffee table. With my sister watching, it's a little easier to be brave and send the damn text I've been wanting to send for days.

Me: How's it going?

She replies just a couple quick minutes later, much to my delight. I am not all about waiting anxiously.

Jenn: I'm good. School sucks. How are you?

Me: My arm hurts

Jenn: lol, sorry! Just a few weeks left and you'll be good as new.

Me: You busy tonight? My sister was just telling me about the fall festival

Jenn: I haven't been to that in forever! I kind of forgot about it.

Me: Want to go? :)

Jenn: That would be fun

Another throw pillow smacks me in the face. I look up to see Bella grinning at me. "You don't look like it's just *fake*," she says in her annoying teasing little sister voice.

I realize I've been smiling this whole time, like a total loser. Ugh.

I throw the pillow back at her. Another text from Jenn comes in.

Jenn: I don't think anyone noticed our first fake date. No one has said anything to me, so maybe this one will work.

It's hard not to be disappointed. I was hoping she'd say she was looking forward to seeing me again, but instead she's all business. I suck it up and reply in the same way.

Me: There will probably be a lot more people at the festival. I'm sure word will get out about your awesome new "boyfriend." :)

Jenn: I hope so! Want to meet there around 7?

Me: I could pick you up?

Jenn: Nah, that's okay. I live pretty close to the festival grounds. I'll just see you there

I guess that's for the best, because I don't exactly have a car here. At best, I'd have to pick her up in my sister's car with my sister in the backseat. That would be a dick move. Bella is so excited about her new car and she should be the one to drive it. The fact that I don't even have a car here is evidence enough that this fake relationship will only ever be fake.

I realize Bella's watching me expectantly.

I shrug. "She said she'll meet me at the festival."

"Cool," Bella says. "The whole town will be there, so be prepared to have a lot of eyes on you."

"I'm used to that," I say. And it's true in a way. I'm used to motocross fame. Not exactly used to being stared at because I'm dating a local. This should be fun.

WHEN SIX-THIRTY ROLLS AROUND, I shower and get dressed and attempt to do something with my hair. I'm a little nervous, which is completely stupid. There's no reason to be nervous about a fake girlfriend. I don't have to worry about impressing her because she's not here to be impressed, she's here to make her ex mad.

Still, I try to look as good as I can in dark jeans and a black button-up shirt, my sleeves rolled a few times to my mid forearm.

Bella seems to approve. "You look hot," she says, curling her lip as she walks past me in the living room. "All my friends will be swooning over you all night. Ugh."

I chuckle and Grandma comes up and puts an arm around my shoulders. She's ridiculously shorter than I am.

"I think you look real handsome," she says, leaning up on her toes to give me a kiss on the cheek.

"Thanks, Grandma."

I don't think Bella has told her anything about my fake relationship, and I certainly haven't, but she winks at me as she walks back to the couch and I wonder if she somehow knows.

I let Bella drive us to the festival, both because she knows the way and it's her car. It's weird, this new dynamic where my baby sister is all grown up. But it's cool. She's becoming an awesome person.

We park in a huge field that's become a makeshift parking

lot, and I buy both of us wristbands that let us have unlimited rides all night.

The place is packed. The smell of fair food fills the air and makes my mouth water. There's a BBQ cookoff going on tonight, so the smells are even better than usual. There's no trace of funnel cake in the air. It's dusk, and the bright lights of the carnival rides sparkle against the dark blue sky.

Bella and I walk toward the Ferris wheel where she's supposed to meet up with her friends. I'm looking for Jenn but haven't seen her yet. Unlike Bella and her friends, Jenn and I didn't set up a meeting place beforehand. I want to text her, but I also want to play it cool.

"Oh my God!" The girly shriek comes from the teenager who just hugged my sister. "You're Aiden Strauss!" she says, her piercing blue eyes boring into me. She puts a hand to her chest. "I'm a huge fan."

"Cool, nice to meet you," I say.

The girl looks at Bella and then back to me. "Can we, like, get a picture together?"

I grin. "Sure."

More of Bella's friends show up at their designated meeting spot, and I take a few photos and listen to them gush about how much they love watching me ride. I know they would say that to any professional motocross racer they met, but it's still cool to hear. Bella and her friends get in line for the Ferris wheel, and I stay behind, keeping my eye out for the girl I'm pretend dating.

I check my phone, and there's nothing there.

When Bella jostles off the Ferris wheel several minutes later, she's all smiles with her friends. She grabs my arm. "You don't have to hang out with us," she says. "Go find Jenn."

Now that she's cut me loose, I feel remarkably lonely. But I also can't tag along with my teenage sister and her merry band of fangirls because that's just lame.

So I start walking around, keeping my eyes open for the girl that's been on my mind all week.

I stroll around to the livestock area, which has a petting zoo and beautifully groomed animals on display, some of them sporting blue ribbons. I guess it's some kind of livestock judging contest.

I lean over a fence and pet a black and white cow. Then, in the distance, I see her.

At least, I'm pretty sure it's her. Her brown hair is tied in that high bun hairstyle she does, and she's got her back to me, but I think I'd recognize her ass anywhere. I mean, it's perfect, after all.

I pat the cow one last time and then make my way across the hay-covered ground to where she's standing in line at a beer truck.

As I get closer, I can tell she's not alone. I don't even think she's standing in line to get a beer, she's just standing near the line.

She shakes her head and puts a hand on her hip. That's when I notice the guy standing in front of her. He's got blond hair cropped short and shaved high on the sides, a stocky build, and the face of a douchebag if I've ever seen one. He's wearing jeans and flip-flops and I mentally roll my eyes at that fashion choice. Jenn shakes her head again and turns to walk away.

The guy grabs her arm, making her stay put.

Oh hell no. I walk faster, weaving through people as I make my way up to her. The guy notices me first. His eyes go wide, and that pissed off expression he'd had a moment before disappears. "Dude, are you Aiden Strauss?" he says.

I slide my arm around Jenn's shoulders, choosing not to answer his question. "Is there a problem here?"

TWELVE

Jenn

THE WHOLE WORLD SEEMS TO STOP FOR JUST A SECOND. All the festival sounds of livestock and obnoxious carnies and rowdy, drunk people just go away—if only in my own mind. It is dead silent. For just a moment.

Jay's excited expression slides off his face, and he looks from Aiden's arm that's now firmly around my shoulder, to me, and back.

"You two know each other?" he says. His knuckles go white as they grip his beer bottle.

Aiden looks down at me, a cute and smug grin appearing on his lips. "Yeah, we've met," he says. The soft tone of his voice sends a shiver down my spine. Damn, he's good at faking this whole boyfriend thing.

"Ah, cool," Jay says. "Dude, it's so cool to meet you! I'm a huge fan."

Aiden quirks an eyebrow, and I probably look exactly the same way. It dawns on me that Jay is too damn dense to realize Aiden was just totally flirting with me. His sexy smile and protective arm around me was his way of saying *she's with me, so back off.*

But Jay didn't even pick up on it.

Oh my God, how did I date someone this stupid for so long?

"Uh, thanks," Aiden says. He's clearly as taken aback by Jay's fanboy-ing as I am.

Jay shifts his beer to the other hand and holds it out to shake Aiden's hand. "It's good to meet you, man. I heard you were in town."

Aiden holds up his cast as an excuse to get out of shaking hands with my ex. Jay is undeterred, and he starts talking about how he watched Aiden's wreck that broke his wrist on TV. He's going on and on, talking all excitedly because he's just met one of his idols. Which is really stupid because they are the same age. Is your idol supposed to be the same age as you? I don't think so.

I can see a muscle flex in Aiden's jaw while he politely answers Jay's questions. He gives me a questioning glance, and I can tell he's wondering if this is the ex-boyfriend he's supposed to be making jealous, because if so, it's not working.

I give a slight nod. Jay keeps talking, trying to brag about his race times at the local track. He's saying how he wants to go pro too and that he just needs to find a sponsor.

Okay, that's enough of this shit.

I clear my throat, and put a hand on Aiden's arm. I give him my flirtiest look, and I might even bat my eyelashes a little. I need this to be crystal clear for Jay's tiny ass brain to comprehend.

"Aiden, will you buy me a drink?" I flash him a sweet smile.

"Sure thing, babe," Aiden says, meeting my smile with one of his own. He turns to Jay. "If you'll excuse us," he says.

Jay's eyes widen, his jaw gritting tight. Okay, now he gets it. Finally.

"What the hell?" he says, taking a step back. "He motions

his hand in front of us. "What the hell is this? You trying to take my girl?"

I can feel Aiden's bicep stiffen under my hand, which is still resting on it. "I didn't have to try very hard," Aiden says. "It turns out treating women with respect is a great way to get their attention."

A vein in Jay's forehead bulges. His fists tighten at his sides. "You wanna talk shit again?" he says, bowing up to Aiden.

This is not good. Aiden has a broken wrist and he definitely doesn't need to get into a fight right now. Plus, there are cops everywhere and I'm sure both of them could get arrested on the spot for assault or disturbing the peace or something.

Aiden doesn't seem concerned, though. In fact, he relaxes a little. He looks right at Jay. "Walk away."

"Man, screw this," Jay says, bouncing on the balls of his feet. He's all reared up and ready to throw punches and I can tell it's pissing him off that Aiden isn't doing the same thing. "You can't come in here and take my girl and get away with it. I don't care how famous you are."

"You need to walk away now," Aiden says. His voice is hard, despite his casual demeanor, and his words send a chill down my spine. Jay must feel the same way because with one last bitter glance at me, he turns and leaves.

"Holy shit," I breathe after he's gone.

Aiden's cast feels scratchy and hard against my back as he wraps his arm around me again.

"You can do so much better than him," Aiden says, softly pressing a kiss to the top of my head. "Let's get a drink."

I think both of us are sick of standing in front of this beer truck, so we make our way down toward the main food area of the festival. There's a place that sells margaritas in every flavor you can think of, and I order a peach one, frozen. Aiden gets the regular lime, on the rocks.

I reach for the cash in my pocket and Aiden shakes his head. "It's on me."

"But you bought our food last time," I argue.

He grins. "What a coincidence, I'm also buying it this time."

I roll my eyes as he hands his card to the lady in the margarita food truck. She points her finger at me. "He's a keeper, honey."

I blush, and I think back to all the times Jay and I split our bills together. A long time ago he'd said it would be unfair for the guy to pay for everything, so we took turns paying for meals when we went out. Now that Aiden has paid twice in a row, it's really sweet, but I feel awkward. Like I owe him now.

We find an unoccupied bench in front of the Ferris Wheel, and I hurry and claim it before someone else does. Aiden laughs. "You don't want to walk around?" he says, sitting next to me.

I shake my head. "I feel like I need some quiet calm time to get what just happened out of my head."

"Calm time and tequila," Aiden says, holding out his plastic cup.

I knock mine to his in a toast. "Amen. I can't believe he tried to fight you. You have a broken wrist. It's not like it'd be a fair fight."

He shrugs. "I can't exactly fight him without a broken wrist, either. Team Loco would kill me."

"Shit, I didn't think of that."

He grins and tucks a strand of hair that had fallen out of my bun behind my ear. "Well, they wouldn't *kill* me. But I'd most definitely get fired. And then finding a new race team would be hard."

"Thanks for all of that," I say, swallowing. I sit back against the cool metal bench seat and watch the lights of the carnival rides as they flicker and swirl. "You're doing more than enough to help me. I really appreciate it."

"I'm happy to," he says, his voice soft.

I glance over at him and he's gazing off into the distance too. His jawline looks sexy under the glow of the lights. The sun has pretty much set now, and the sky is a deep blue, illuminated by moonlight. Aiden looks so gorgeous right now. I can't help myself.

I scoot over a little, until we're right next to each other, and then I rest my head on his shoulder. Aiden takes a long sip of his margarita, finishing it off, then he tosses the empty cup ten feet through the air. It lands perfectly in a nearby trashcan.

He puts his arm around me and we sit like this for a long moment. I can smell his cologne, all woodsy and manly, and hear the beating of his heart. All around us, people are having a good time at the festival. This is nice. This is the best time I've had in a while.

Of course, it's also fake. My heart squeezes. I'm still thinking about that kiss the other day and how much it took out of me. I'd liked it so much. I needed it. I wanted it. And that's not okay. The last thing I need to do after having my heart broken is fall for a guy I can't have.

I sit up.

"I feel like we need to set some ground rules," I say. "Like... iron out the details of this fake relationship."

Aiden's brow quirks. "Is this about the ball pit kiss?"

My cheeks go warm. I nod. "Kind of. I mean...I think we should only do PDA type stuff if it's for an audience...like to get our point across."

"Sure," Aiden says with a nod. "I understand."

"Maybe even only in front of Jay or something," I add. "Of course, we probably reached our goal tonight but... I want to make him extra jealous. I want him to think we're dating for a long time and that it's not just some one night fling."

"I totally agree," Aiden says. "That was fun earlier, but it wasn't enough."

I smile. "Okay so... no private making out," I reiterate, even though it causes me physical pain to do so. I want to kiss him so badly, but I need to protect my heart first.

"No private making out," Aiden agrees.

Even though it's totally my idea, it sucks that he agrees to it so easily. I guess a tiny stupid part of me hoped he would have fought back and suggested that we make out for fun in private, too. Of course that would be a bad thing. So I tell myself to stop being such an idiot.

I finish my margarita, and either that drink is strong, or I'm a lightweight because I can already feel my body warming and loosening up. I aim my cup toward the trashcan, moving my hand back and forth. Then I sigh. "There's no way I'll make that throw," I say with a laugh that sounds a lot like a giggle in my tipsy state.

"I got you," Aiden says, holding out his left hand. I give him the cup and he makes another perfect throw right into the trashcan.

"You're so skilled," I say, pretending to swoon. But I don't have to pretend very hard.

He laughs. "You're a little drunk."

"No!" I protest, but then he gives me the cutest look and I burst into giggles. "Okay maybe just a little."

Aiden's grin is the cutest thing ever. "My little lightweight girlfriend," he says. "I better keep an eye on you."

"Psh." I wave his worries away with my hand. "I'm good."

He watches me, his lips curved up in a smile, and I feel my insides turn to actual mush. I don't know how he does that, with his charm and ridiculously good looks. It's hard to keep my hands off him normally, and now that tequila is flowing through my veins, it's practically a herculean task.

"Hey," I say, reaching out and touching his chest just for a second. "I have a question."

When I move my hand off his chest, he grabs it and folds his fingers in mine. "Go for it."

I swallow, remembering what my ex-boyfriend had told me. The thing that's been bugging me nonstop. "Do guys have sex because they can't help it?"

Aiden's smile turns to confusion. "Huh?"

"Like... if a girl wants to have sex with you, do you just do it without even thinking?"

His brows narrow. "If that were the case, I would be having a lot of sex on race days."

"So... are you saying you're picky? Like, you'll only choose which girls to sleep with?"

"Jenn, where did this come from?"

I shrug. "Jay said he only slept with Miranda because she threw herself at him. And that guys are just horny sex machines, and they can't help it. He said it was like... I don't know, entrapment."

Aiden's lips flatten. "Jenn, love, that is not true. Not at all."

I shake my head. "I mean, it makes sense. Guys always want sex and they don't care who it's with. So like, I guess I'm asking can you love one girl but sleep with another because you can't help it?"

"Hell no," Aiden says. He straightens and I see a muscle twitch in his jaw. "Absolutely not. Guys like sex, but guys also know how to be in a committed relationship. Jenn, he's an asshole. He's a liar and a cheater and don't let him fool you into thinking anything else."

I frown and gaze off at a group of teenagers in the distance. Aiden squeezes my hand. "Listen to me, Jenn. He's completely wrong. Real men would never cheat on their girlfriend. Not ever. Not accidentally."

I swallow down the lump in my throat. "I guess that's good to know. It's not that he couldn't help it. I just wasn't good enough."

"Come here," Aiden says. He leans over and wraps me in his arms. I let my head rest against his chest as a breeze carries the smell of greasy food through the air. I'm not exactly sad. I guess I'm just exhausted. "Why are guys so shitty?" I ask.

Aiden kisses the top of my hair again. "When you meet the right guy, he won't be shitty at all."

THIRTEEN

Aiden

Jenn is cute when she's tipsy. She's not as guarded, and a little more flirtatious. I like it. What I don't like is the bullshit line her ex gave her about having sex. Does he really think he can lie like that and make her believe it? How many other girls has he told this to?

He's doing a huge disservice to the entire male species by making us look like a bunch of cavemen who are incapable of self-restraint. Not only that, but I certainly don't want to hook up with every girl I come across. Men aren't inherently hard-wired like that. We can be loyal and faithful. I've had so many girls throw themselves at me at the races and I haven't hooked up with a single one. Why? Because sex is more than just sex. It's called making love for a reason.

I want to be with someone important to me. Not just some rando girl who wants to jump my bones. I take a calming breath and look out over the festival grounds, trying to stop feeling so pissed off. That moment is gone. I told Jenn that her ex was lying his ass off and I think she believed me. If not, I'll have to keep finding ways to convince her that not all men are cheating assholes. I don't want her to go falling for another asshat like that again. She deserves someone better. A real man. *Me*, if I wasn't so unavailable because of my career.

We are still sitting on this bench, relaxing against each other while the world goes on, while couples hold hands and little kids scream on rides. A country music band plays under a pavilion to a hundred fans who are dancing along and singing every word. Everyone is having a good time here, but I'm probably having the best time.

Even though she's my fake girlfriend.

I catch the sight of something in the corner of my eye and it gives me an idea. "Hey, Jenn?" I ask.

She lifts her head off my shoulder to look at me. "Yeah?"

"Remember how we said we would save the PDA for times when it would make a difference?"

She nods. I grin. "I'm going to kiss you now."

Her eyes light up in confusion but I crush my lips to hers before she can say anything. Her hand presses hungrily to my chest, sliding up to my neck while her lips move against mine.

The kiss is hot and fruity from her peach margarita and I wish it could last forever. But I might be about to get punched, so I pull away slowly.

"How dare you," she says playfully, her eyes dancing under the glow of the festival lights.

I lean forward and whisper in her ear, "We have an audience."

She looks over her shoulder. Jay is standing not twenty feet away, holding a corndog and wearing the angriest look of contempt I've ever seen on a man. He shakes his head in disgust and stalks off.

Jenn giggles. "Okay, that was amazing."

I brush some hair out of her eyes and grin down at her. I want to kiss her so badly, but I promised I'd only do that if we had a captive audience. No one is watching us right now. Kissing her would be against the rules.

I can feel my pants tightening in arousal from that kiss. I have to get away from this situation, stat. "Wanna go for a walk?" I ask.

"Sure," she says, and I swear she sounds a little breathless, like maybe she was thinking the same thing.

That only makes my manhood even harder.

I reach over and take her hand. I know it's not as serious as kissing, but it still counts as PDA. I'm afraid she'll rebuke me at first, but she doesn't. Her fingers lace into mine like it's an old habit.

"He's still here," I say as an explanation. "He might run into us again, so I figured we should be holding hands."

She smiles up at me. "I was thinking the same thing."

We wander down the festival, hand in hand, looking exactly like every other happy couple here. I wonder if anyone else is here faking a relationship. Probably not.

"Aiden!" my sister calls out. We find her standing near a guy selling cotton candy. She waves us over. "Hey, Jenn!"

"Hey," Jenn says. She glances up at me.

"She knows the truth," I whisper. "But her friends don't."

Bella tells us we have to try the cotton candy because it's really good, so I buy some for me and Jenn. Bella's friends cluster around me, all taking turns talking about how much they love motocross while we wait for the guy to swirl up a fresh batch of pink cotton candy around the paper handle.

See, this is what happens every time I go anywhere with a motocross scene. Girls flock to me, bat their eyelashes and talk to me about their extensive love of the sport. It's amazing how many of them find a way to casually (but not so casually) touch my arm while they talk. If men were like Jay says they are, then I'd be stripping down and having sex with each girl here.

Of course, I'm not. Which proves my point exactly.

I wish I could tell Jenn that, but I can't exactly say that topic out loud in front of everyone. Still, I'm polite though, because they're fans, and the fans have a lot of sway in professional motocross. Team Loco likes me to maintain a good rapport with them.

Jenn and I tag along with Bella and her friends for a while. I'm happy for the extra people because it's helping me focus on not being attracted to Jenn. When it's just the two of us, I find myself wanting to do all kinds of naughty things with her. We need this buffer of five extra people. Well, at least I need it. I'm sure Jenn is just fine.

The next couple of hours are a blast. Jenn and I ride a ton of rides. I especially love the scarier ones because she clutches onto me and buries her face in my shirt. I get to wrap my arm around her and hold her tightly. We don't run into Jenn's ex anymore, and I'm grateful that we don't have to have the happy mood ruined by that prick. Still, it would have been nice to have an excuse to kiss her again. Regardless, I'm just really happy being here with her. It's also nice spending time with my little sister.

Half an hour before the festival closes for the night, we all decide to ride the Ferris Wheel before going home. Luckily, it's the kind that only has room for two people per seat, unlike those bigger ones that fit four people in each carriage. Jenn and I get to be alone.

She snuggles against me, like she's done all night. I might love it more than I love kissing her. She's soft and warm and makes my heart all melty when she's near me. I love the smell of her and the feel of her hair through my fingers.

I close my eyes and breathe in the moment while the ride takes off, swooping us to the top of the wheel and then back down again.

All of a sudden I hear the screech of fireworks. Jenn and I look up and see a burst of red sparkle through the sky.

"There's fireworks?" I say.

"Every night during the festival," she says.

"Sweet."

We have the perfect vantage point to see the fireworks as they go off while we ride the Ferris Wheel. Soon, the ride is almost over, but the colorful sparkles are still lighting up the sky. We get stopped at the very top while they let off some passengers below.

"This was really fun," Jenn says. Her eyes light up blue from a firework.

"Yeah it was. This is the first time I've done something that wasn't work in a long time."

Her eyes sparkle again. "Thanks for everything."

"Trust me, the pleasure was mine."

My phone goes off, halfway ruining the moment. Our ride jostles forward a few feet while the next person at the bottom of the wheel gets off. It's Bella texting me.

"My sister wants to go to her friend's house after this," I tell Jenn. "But she forgot she has to drive me home."

I'm about to type out a reply when Jenn puts a hand over mine. "I'll take you home," she says softly.

"No, I don't want you to do that. It's out of the way."

She shrugs one shoulder. "Okay so maybe you should just come home with me?"

I swallow.

She watches me for so long I think I might explode from anticipation. "You want me to come over?" I say.

She grins. "We could hang out. You know... as friends."

"Okay, sure," I say with a nod. "That would be fun."

A final blast of color fills the night sky. Jenn's eyes crinkle at the corners. And then she grabs my shirt and pulls me toward her. Her eyes close, and mine do too.

And then we're kissing once more, with no one around to see us.

It certainly doesn't feel like we're just friends.

FOURTEEN

Jenn

I PUSH AIDEN AWAY, WHICH IS STUPID BECAUSE I WAS THE one who pulled him to me in the first place. I slide backward in the small ride seat, feeling ten times more flustered than I am tipsy. I mean seriously, it was one margarita. I shouldn't be this... swoony.

Aiden puts a hand on the back of his neck as he watches me with curious eyes. Shit. Why did I do that? Why did I kiss him? All night he's been acting like the world's greatest boyfriend and I just couldn't help myself.

For a second, I think about lying and saying I saw Jay standing in line for the Ferris wheel and that's why I kissed him. *It was just Jay! It wasn't me losing my mind over how handsome you are!*

But I know I'm not that good of a liar, so I just shrug. "Sorry about that," I say as the ride stops at the bottom and we get off.

Aiden laughs. "Give me your keys. You are way too drunk to drive."

Ah, perfect. Drunk. Yes. That's why he thinks I kissed him. I'll just go along with that idea.

I nod and hand him my truck keys. I even sway a little as I

walk out of the fairgrounds, just to keep up with the drunk girl act.

Am I pathetic? Yes.

But it's not my fault. I'm being overloaded with the hotness that is Aiden Strauss and it's making my brain short circuit. Ten minutes ago, I'd felt like inviting him to my apartment was the greatest idea in the world.

And well, I still feel like that, only now I'm embarrassed at how pathetic I can be. Aiden doesn't hold my hand while we make our way through the parked cars toward my truck. At least half of the crowd has already left, so the parking lot—which is actually a field—is easier to navigate.

"This is me," I say, pointing to my shiny new pickup truck.

"Nice wheels," Aiden says, unlocking the door with my key fob. He pulls open the passenger door and holds it out for me. At first I think he's being romantic but then he reaches out a hand to help me climb inside and I remember that he thinks I'm drunk. "I bet it was a big change going from the Camaro to this," he says.

"Yeah, but it was worth it. I can take my bike to the track without asking someone else to load it for me."

He nods, an approving smile tugging at his lips. I look away, pretending to fidget with my purse, because I don't trust myself to meet his gaze right now. I'm too scared I'll reveal my secrets—that I'm totally into him, and not in a fake way.

He jogs over to the driver's side and starts my truck. He looks good in a truck. Sexy as hell, actually.

We don't talk much on the drive, and I'm impressed that Aiden remembers how to get to my house on these old back roads. Lately I seem to be impressed by everything he does. Maybe that's just the messed up part of my brain talking.

Once we're back home, I know my alcohol has worn off. I'm

thinking clearly now, and my heart is racing, because I know exactly what I want to do.

Luckily, my apartment is clean, even cleaner than usual after I went on my post-breakup cleaning spree. I let Aiden inside and I lock the door behind us. I'm pretty sure my parents are asleep now, but if my dad happened to see Aiden get here, he'd want to come say hi.

Nothing would kill the mood faster than that.

"Nice place," Aiden says as his gaze lingers across my living room. The living room and kitchen are kind of one big space and then there's a hallway off to the side that leads to my bedroom and bathroom. It's small, only the size of a three car garage, but it's home.

"My dad and I built the place," I say, holding my arms open wide to gesture to my masterpiece.

"Yeah?" Aiden says, quirking an eyebrow. "Impressive."

"We had to hire an electrician and plumber but we did everything else. Dad used to hang drywall in his younger years. I took so many trips to Home Depot that year that I now never want to go back again," I say with a laugh.

Aiden smiles. "I've never moved out on my own." He sits on the couch and I join him, keeping a few inches of space between us. "I know that sounds pathetic," he goes on, "But I've been racing every weekend since I turned eighteen and there's just never been time or reason to move out. I spend most of my time with Team Loco now, living in hotels. And when I come home it's only for a few weeks so I just stay at my parent's place. Luckily it's big enough that I normally don't have to see anyone."

"That seems like a crazy life," I say. I run my fingers up and down the groove in the couch cushion while I talk. "Always being on the road and stuff."

He nods. "It's fun and amazing and it pays well but there's a downside."

It seems like he's going to keep talking, so when he doesn't, I look up at him. He's watching me with an intensity that sends a shiver down my spine. "The major downside is that I can't have relationships."

"You could..." I say, feeling my throat go dry. "It would just be different."

He shrugs. "It's hard on all relationships. I haven't seen my sister in forever. I didn't even know she had moved down here. I never see my mom. I haven't had a girlfriend in so long I—" He stops. Shakes his head. "Never mind. Let's only talk about fun stuff tonight."

His hand is resting on the couch just inches from mine. I can almost feel the spark of electricity dancing between our fingers. Maybe it's all in my mind?

But as I stare at our hands, Aiden slides his over, his fingertips covering mine. I look up and find him watching me.

"I had fun tonight," he says, his voice deep and sexier than usual. "I'm starting to think that breaking my wrist wasn't the worst thing ever."

I can't help but grin, and I bite down on the inside of my lip to stop myself from grinning too much. "I'm glad you had fun," I say, trying to keep it cool.

Why did I even invite him over? I know why—I didn't want the night to end. And...maybe I wanted something else, too. Maybe my subconscious told me to invite him over so that we could—

My heart pounds. I know what I'm going to do, and it scares me, but it's too late to back out now. I look up. "Wanna make out?"

Aiden's fingers wrap around mine. He glances around. "But we're not in public."

I shrug one shoulder. "It can be practice."

His grin widens. His tongue flicks across his bottom lip and the flutters in my stomach go into overdrive.

"Practice is important," he says, inching closer to me. His good hand reaches up and slides behind my neck as he leans toward me.

I nod slowly. "Practice is good."

He kisses me. For the third time tonight I feel the rush of warmth spreading through my body when his lips touch mine. This time, it's different. It's not just a quick kiss that ends a few seconds later, leaving me wanting more.

This time, I take more. I lean in, kissing him again, and again, my tongue clashing with his as our kisses become passionate. At some point, I realize I'm sitting in his lap and I don't even know how I got here. I feel his cast pressed against my back while his good hand slides up my arm and tucks behind my hair.

When I lightly pull away to gasp for air, Aiden kisses my neck. I freeze, unaccustomed to how good that can feel. His lips dance across the sensitive skin, trailing kisses down to my collarbone. My breathing gets shallow.

"Should I stop?" Aiden whispers, his breath hot on my neck.

I shake my head. "No."

He grins, then kisses my collar, neck, cheek, and lips.

I grab his face and draw him in, willing our ravenous kisses to fill the need inside of me. But it only does so much. I need way much more than this.

I stand up and take his hand. It doesn't escape my notice that his jeans have gotten a lot tighter in the crotch, and the sight of it turns me on even more.

"Let's go," I say.

He doesn't question me. He just follows me to my bedroom. I'm a little hesitant on what to do next, but I try to act confident. Sex with Jay was formulaic. He'd tell me to strip, and I would take off my clothes quickly. We'd get on the bed and do it—often finishing in just a few minutes. Sex was never really fun with Jay, no matter how hard I tried to make it worthwhile. But Jay also didn't kiss like Aiden.

I bite my lip as I stand next to my bed. This plan had felt so right but now I'm not sure what to do next. Then Aiden's hands are on my hips, and he brings his toes right up to mine, his forehead dropping down as he places one soft kiss on my lips.

"How drunk are you?" he asks.

"I'm not drunk," I say, looking him right in the eyes so he knows I'm serious. I wrap my arms around his shoulders and peer up at him, unable to hide my smile.

"I don't want you to regret this," he whispers.

I shake my head. "I won't."

When he doesn't look convinced, I lean up on my toes and kiss his neck. I feel a soft groan escape his lips and I press my body up against his, feeling his hardened desire pressing against my belly.

It feels good to know I'm turning him on. I run my tongue up his neck and his good hand squeezes my hip. "Holy shit," he breathes.

I giggle and kiss his ear, then kiss back down his neck, giving him the same torture he gave me a minute ago.

Then I spin him around and sit him on the edge of my bed, pressing down on his shoulders until he obeys me. Now, with him sitting and me standing, I'm slightly taller than he is and I'm so turned on I can't possibly find any shyness inside of me.

I pull off my shirt. I chose my sexiest bra today, not that I knew it'd be seen, but I'm so glad I did. It pushes up my boobs and makes them look awesome, and now they're right in Aiden's face.

With one hand, he pulls off his own shirt and tosses it on top of mine on the floor. I swallow, feeling my heart pound as I take in the sight of his sculpted chest and tanned skin. I run my fingers down his chest and then back up to his shoulders. He watches me admiring him, and I take my time, placing a kiss on his lips before I stand back up. His good hand slides up my belly, sending a shiver down my spine, only stopping when he cups my breast. He squeezes it, gently, but enough to make heat blossom between my legs. Okay, screw going slow. I unbutton my shorts and let them fall to the ground.

Aiden's gaze drifts down my body, and for once I feel appreciated, like he's taking in every inch of me and he likes what he sees. I've never felt that way before.

I step closer, grabbing his shoulders. "Off with the pants," I say, like I'm some kind of sexy queen of hearts.

His tongue flicks across his bottom lip, but he does what he's told, standing up and removing his jeans. Now we're both in our underwear, his arousal showing through his red boxer briefs. For a split second, I'm not sure what to do. I want to be sexy and confident, but what's next? Do I grab the condom from my nightstand drawer and hand it to him?

He must notice the hesitation on my face because he circles his arms around me, holding me close like we're slow dancing. "We don't have to go any farther," he whispers into my ear.

"But I want to," I whisper back.

I feel his fingers trailing up my back. "Stop me at any time," he says softly before pressing his lips to my neck. "I won't mind."

I nod, my throat dry. Then I feel my bra slip free. He must have unbuckled the back without me even noticing. I slide my arms out of the straps and let it fall.

Aiden cups my breasts as much as his cast will allow him, but at least his fingers are free to flick over my nipples. He sits back down on the bed, bringing me with him until I'm standing between his legs, my bare breasts right in his face. He brings a nipple into his mouth and flicks his tongue across it, looking up to meet my gaze. I bite my lip because I'm afraid I'll cry out way too loudly if I don't. The pleasure is intoxicating as he licks my nipple and then brings his mouth to the other one. I close my eyes, my breathing coming in gasps.

When he pulls away this time, he leans up and kisses me on the mouth next. I wrap my arms around his shoulders and stand as close as I can with him sitting on the bed.

"There's condoms in the nightstand," I manage to say. My toes curl up and I don't know how much longer I can stand here without begging him to hurry up.

"That can wait a little while longer," Aiden breathes, his lips against mine. He gives me the sexiest look. "I'm not even close to being done with the foreplay."

FIFTEEN

Aiden

My phone rings at the ass crack of dawn. I roll over in bed, get all tangled up in Grandma's quilt, and have to fight with it before my arm is free to reach for my phone. For the smallest second, I allow myself to hope that it might be Jenn.

But the man on the other line, with his gruff voice and annoying cheerfulness is not her.

"What's up, man?" Marcus says, sounding like he's been awake for hours, which he probably has. I check the time—nine in the morning—and yawn.

"Not much," I say, sitting up in bed. The sheets are a tangled mess, probably because I didn't sleep well last night. I haven't slept well in the last three nights.

"How many weeks we got left until that wrist is healed?" my manager asks.

"Four," I say. "That's when the cast comes off but I'll have to ask a doctor when I'll be cleared to ride again."

"You'll probably need to wait a couple weeks after that, but you could at least get back with the team by then."

I nod. "Yep, I'm looking forward to it."

For a very short while I had allowed myself to think that I

enjoyed living here. That staying in the same place was fun because you could make friends, memories. But now I think I'm ready to get back to my crazy life of travel.

I had only *thought* I'd made friends. What I really made was an agreement.

I chat with Marcus for a little while longer, and then when we get off the phone, I'm no longer in the mood to sleep. I can smell bacon cooking in the kitchen and I wonder if Grandma always cooks a nice breakfast or if she's just doing it because we're in town.

I stare at my phone, watching the screen remain blank and empty. Devoid of any calls. Saturday could have just been a busy day. Sunday—maybe she had to be with family or something. But now it's Monday and if Jenn doesn't talk to me then my fears will be confirmed.

Having sex with her was a really, *really* bad idea.

Don't get me wrong, it was amazing that night. I've never felt so close to anyone in my whole life. I even allowed myself to drop the fake boyfriend act and to treat her as if she were really mine. I thought she liked it. She certainly acted like she liked it. The way she moaned and called out my name, the way her back arched as I slid into her.

It was sexy as hell. It was the best night ever.

And then, after cuddling in her bed for an hour, I had done the nice thing and said I better get back home. I was hoping, praying, that she'd tell me to spend the night. Instead, she said, "I'll drive you home."

On the short drive back to my house, we'd talked about any and everything—laughing and joking around all topics except the topic of sex. It's like we just pretended that mind-blowing night didn't happen.

And then, just before dropping me off, Jenn had looked over at me and called my name.

"Yes?" I said, peering back into her truck while I stood in the driveway.

"All of that stuff was just as friends," she said. "It didn't mean anything."

I swallowed, and nodded. "Of course."

Then she smiled and waved goodbye. I felt a little punched in the face, but her smile made everything okay. I knew that night wasn't real—none of it is real—but it's not like she needed to remind me.

And now I haven't heard from her at all. I can't stop wondering that I did something wrong. I've gone through the whole night in my head, and it seems like it was just a great night together. I didn't do anything she didn't want me to. The only thing I did wrong was pretend that she was my actual girlfriend in my mind. But it's not like she knows that.

Still, I'm being set aside now and it sucks. Jenn and I had started texting each other all the time, like friends. I want to text her so badly but I don't know what to say.

I eat breakfast with my grandma and sister, and I'm able to put on a happy face to chat with them. Then Grandma goes out to her garden and Bella takes her laptop to the couch to get started on her school work, and I'm all alone again.

I sit next to Bella, but I don't want to disturb her studies. I'm sure if I mentioned that I'm having problems with Jenn, she'd be all ears, but she needs to focus right now.

I head outside and walk down the long winding driveway, making sure I'm very far away from Grandma's garden so she can't overhear me. I call Jett. He's on Team Loco and he's been in a long-term relationship for a while now.

"What's up?" Jett says. In the background I can hear the rumble of a dirt bike and it makes my chest ache to be back on the track again.

"You got a minute?"

"For you? Always," he says sarcastically.

I feel like an idiot, but I tell him the whole story with Jenn. I tell him we hooked up on Friday and I spare him the details about how amazing it was. He just needs the facts.

When I'm finished recounting the last couple of weeks he says, "So what's the problem, dude? You fell for her, huh?"

"No," I say, knowing it's a lie. "I mean, I thought we were friends. Now she's not even talking to me."

"Sex will do that," Jett says. "It's the one thing that turns friends into something else."

"So what should I do?"

He considers it for a moment. "Well, you could tell her how you feel."

"I can't do that," I say, shaking my head. "What's the point? I don't even live here."

"Long distance can work if you want it to," Jett says. "But if you don't want a relationship with her and you're just going to leave in a few weeks, maybe you shouldn't do anything."

That's not the advice I wanted to hear. "That's the best you've got?" I say.

He chuckles. "Man, you either go for it and tell her you want to date her for real, or you realize that you *don't* want to date her for real—because of the long distance or whatever your reason is—and if that's the case then you need to just let it go. No sense in stringing her along, ya know?"

"Yeah... I get it."

He's right. I know he is. She clearly doesn't feel the same way about me that I feel about her. Telling her I'm crazy about her—in a real way, not a fake way—would only put her in a bad position.

I thank Jett for his advice and then we chat about the races for a bit. He's still holding his first place position on the team, but Zach is in second with Clay in third. Apparently, Clay's bike had a piston malfunction in the last race and he didn't get to finish the race.

When we're finished talking, I walk back to the house feeling only slightly better. I know Jett is right. This whole thing with Jenn started out as pretend. Just because I wanted there to be more doesn't mean I'll get it. And it would be wrong anyway. Jenn lives here, and has her life here. I don't technically have a home anywhere. I just need to get over her.

I head to the gym and get a good workout, and then I come home around dinner time. I didn't see Jenn at the gym, but I'd also made sure not to look over at the PT area. I figured if she was there and she wanted to talk to me then she could be the one to make that choice.

At home, Bella is ordering pizza delivery. "You want some?" she asks.

"What I want is a drink," I say.

She lifts an eyebrow. "They don't sell alcohol at the pizza place."

I laugh. "Is there a bar around here?"

"You okay?" she asks, tilting her head.

"Yeah, I just miss motocross," I lie. "I talked to the guys today and it's got me bummed out. I could use a drink."

"Well the only bar around here is pretty gross but there's the Mexican food place over on Maple and half the restaurant is a bar. People say they make the best drinks."

"Perfect," I say. "You wanna come with me?"

She shakes her head. "It's Monday night, which means my favorite show comes on and Grandma and I always order pizza and watch it."

"Boring," I say, teasing her.

She rolls her eyes. "You can take my car if you want to go, but you shouldn't drink alone."

"I won't," I say, which is also a lie.

"Ohh," Bella says, wiggling her eyebrows. "I forgot about your fake girlfriend."

I just let her think what she's going to think and I head out alone. The truth is, I am definitely drinking alone tonight.

The restaurant is packed, even though this is a fairly small town. I find a spot at the bar and order a Jack and Coke. That's a sad person's drink, and I'm pretty pitiful right now.

"I'll have what he's having," a girl says as she slides onto the barstool next to me.

She looks over at me, flicking her dark hair over her shoulder. "Hey there, sexy."

I give her a nod of acknowledgment and take the glass the bartender slides over to me.

"You're new," the girl says. "You're probably the hottest guy in this place."

"Uh, thanks?" I say, taking a sip of my drink. The liquor burns down my throat, warming me. Once I finish this thing, I'll feel two percent better about Jenn.

The girl is staring at me. She's about my age, and she's wearing a thick line of black eyeliner that kind of looks bad. I guess she's pretty enough though. Nothing spectacular. She's not like Jenn. Jenn doesn't have to hang half of her boobs out of a black tank top to get any attention, and this girl clearly does.

When the bartender delivers her drink, she holds the glass out to me for a toast. I'm not going to be rude, so I clink my glass to hers. "To meeting new people," she says, giving me a flirtatious grin. I guess for once it's nice to meet a stranger who isn't a raving motocross fan. She has no idea who I am.

She takes her glass and drinks the whole thing in one shot.

"Damn," I say, impressed.

She grins. "Your turn."

I didn't come here to get drunk, but downing one drink

won't hurt, I guess. I meet her grin with one of my own and then I chug the drink in one go. *Whoosh*.

My glass slaps the bar.

"Another round," she tells the bartender. She puts a hand on my arm. "What's your name?"

"Aiden."

"Hi, Aiden," she says, giving me a flirtatious look. "I'm Miranda. Nice to meet you."

SIXTEEN

Jenn

WHY DOES THE HUMAN BODY HAVE SO MANY PARTS? My anatomy class is kicking my butt. I've been studying all weekend, making up rhymes to help me remember stuff, and I still feel unprepared for tomorrow's exam. And why are we even taking an exam on a Tuesday? That's total crap.

I've always heard that the first two years of college classes are the easiest, and that's right. I've had to study so much more this semester than any other semester so far.

I sit up straighter on my bed, breathe in deeply, and slowly let it out. If yoga breathing doesn't help me calm down, nothing will. I've been sitting cross-legged on my bed, my face buried in my textbook for four hours now. I should probably get up and pee since there's two empty Coke cans on my nightstand. I wanted coffee for the caffeine but it's so hot outside I opted for something cooler.

Shoving the textbook off my lap, I get up and stretch my limbs. My thoughts are a flurry of body parts and muscular systems and nervous systems and all kinds of systems. Way too many. Why are humans so complicated?

After peeing, I head into the kitchen for a snack. But the

fridge is devoid of anything that sounds good and the pantry is just as boring. I need something extremely delicious to get me out of this funk and crackers or chips or apple slices will not do it.

I settle on grabbing another soda and then I head back to my room. As soon as I sit back down, a rush of memories come to me. It's like as soon as I stop thinking about school, Aiden appears. There is not enough room in my mind for both him and schoolwork, so I've been doing my best to stop thinking about him.

My best is apparently not very good.

I look around, and even though my bed is perfectly made right now, I can still remember the sheets getting all disheveled after our amazing night together. A rush of heat swells between my legs at the memories.

No. Not now, Jenn.

I bite hard on the inside of my lip to make myself focus on the task at hand. I need to study. I've been studying all weekend but it's not enough. There's no way I can pass the test right now.

My phone blares to life with Mom's ringtone. I ignored her last three calls so I know I need to pick up, lest she send the police over to my house thinking I'm dead or something.

"Hey, Mom."

"Jenny!" she says, calling me the name that only she uses. "I've been calling and calling. What are you doing?"

"Just studying for school. I have a huge exam tomorrow."

"You took all weekend off work to study," she says. "You should be fine by now."

I sigh into the phone. "I'm nowhere close to being fine. This is a lot of information and I need to learn it all."

"How long have you been studying today?"

I check the clock. Holy shit how is it already six in the evening? "Since eight," I say.

I can practically feel Mom's glare at me through the phone. "That is too much! You're going to get burnt out, honey. You need a break."

"Okay, I'll take a break," I say but I have no intention of actually doing it. If I stop studying, I think of Aiden, and if I think of Aiden it's very hard to remember that we're just friends.

So what if the sex was amazing? I can't get hooked on my fake boyfriend.

"Dad and I are coming to get you," she says. "We're going out to dinner."

I groan, but that actually sounds like a good idea. I'm starving. I think I've only had soda today.

"Okay," I say.

Mom brightens. "We're leaving now, so we'll be in your driveway in thirty seconds."

"Thanks for giving me enough time to get dressed!" I say, hanging up the phone in a rush.

It's just dinner with my parents, so it's no big deal, but I am still wearing my pajamas from last night. I throw on some denim shorts and a T-shirt and then slip into the flip-flops by my front door. When I open it, my dad's truck is sitting in my driveway. It does not take long for your parents to visit you when they live on the same property.

Grabbing my purse, I jog down the stairs and climb in the backseat.

"Oh honey," Mom says, turning to face me from the front seat. "You have dark circles under your eyes! You've been working too hard."

"I'm fine," I say, but I rub my eyes as if that's going to somehow help. If I had time to put on makeup or brush my hair, I would have looked better. But it's not like I'm trying to impress anyone. "Where are we going?"

"Mexican," Dad says.

"Sounds amazing." We have the best Mexican restaurant here, and since most of the other food places are all Cajun seafood, it's nice to have a little variety.

I listen to my parents chat about work and boring stuff for the next ten minutes, but I try to act like a nice daughter who actually cares about this stuff. They're paying for dinner, after all.

In reality, I can't stop thinking about Aiden. He hasn't texted me all weekend, but I didn't really expect him to after I reminded him that we're just friends. I haven't texted him either, for that same reason.

Because I know that if I talk to him, I'll start longing for him, I'll want him to come over. I'll want to lay in his arms and feel his lips on mine.

All of that sounds a hell of a lot like real dating, and I can't do that to myself. My heart has only just healed from an epic heartbreak. I can't go and let it get broken again. No one will take care of my heart except for me.

Aiden and I are friends. And honestly, now that Jay has seen us together, maybe our little fake adventure should be over. It's probably better for my heart if we just end it now.

I'll never be able to watch professional motocross the same way again. Every time I see Aiden on the screen, I'll remember that one glorious night we had together.

At the restaurant, we're taken to a table near the bar, and I can't wait to dive into some chips and queso. My stomach growls like a madman because now that I'm surrounded by the smells of food, I realize how damn hungry I am.

I'm stuffing my face with chips when I hear that laugh. That unmistakable, high pitched, extra annoying sound I've known since high school. Miranda Brown is here.

I grab another chip and try to focus on my parent's conversation. I don't need to look around and see her. I know what she looks like. I've seen way more of her than I ever care to. And she's probably here with Jay, which means he might see us. Oh God. How stupid am I going to look when I'm here with my parents and they're on a romantic date? Not to mention, I look like fifteen year old in a t-shirt and flip-flops with messy hair and no makeup. I've been stressed out over studying, but to Jay it'll look like I'm miserable and heartbroken. My heart races and I keep my head low, hoping they don't see me. If I don't look in their direction then maybe they won't notice me, either. This whole restaurant is pretty packed, so hopefully we just blend into the crowd.

I take a deep breath and let it out slowly. When I hear that insipid laugh again, my instincts make me look in the direction it came from, even though I don't want to see her.

But I do. I see her sitting there at the bar, wearing a tight black dress. She leans over and whispers into a guy's ear. But that guy isn't Jay.

It's Aiden.

I guess I only thought I had protected my heart. Because right now, it hurts bad.

SEVENTEEN

Aiden

"Aiden," I say with a nod. I take a sip of my second drink of the night while some pop song plays overhead, which is an unusual music choice for Mexican restaurant.

Miranda downs half of her second drink in one huge gulp. "Aiden... that's a sexy name."

She reaches over and puts a hand on my leg. She has long natural nails with chipped red polish on them. Her hand looks like it's from a horror film. She squeezes my leg. "Everything about you is sexy," she purrs.

I want to tell her that despite what she thinks, this whole spiel of hers is absolutely not sexy. I guess if I wanted to get laid with a total stranger, all I'd have to do is ask if she wants to go to my car. She'd probably disappear in a cloud of dust, and be waiting for me with her clothes stripped off.

That is not a sexy look at all.

This kind of shit happens all the time when I'm on the road. It's even worse when I'm with the guys, because then a group of girls who are all copies of Miranda will crowd around us, each choosing the guy they want so they can fling themselves on us.

Teenage me would have thought this magnetism to women was the coolest thing ever.

But now all I can see is STDs and waking up next to a stranger that reeks of booze and vomit. Not sexy. Not attractive. Not anything I'm going to do tonight.

I may be hurting over Jenn ghosting me, but I'm not about to trade those feelings for the fleeting touch of some strange woman I just met.

I shift on the barstool and her hand falls away. I have no interest in this girl but I also don't want to be a total asshole to her. I take a menu from the bar and flip through it, acting as if I'm interested in the food. All I wanted to do tonight was have a drink or two alone so that I could try to get over the pain of Jenn ditching me.

"You're the dirt bike guy, right?" Miranda asks.

"Probably," I say. She quirks an eyebrow.

"There are a lot of dirt bike guys in this town since it's home to a motocross track."

She rolls her eyes. "You know what I mean. You're that famous guy everyone's talking about?"

"What are they saying?" I ask.

"Who?" she says, sipping from her drink. Not only is she overly flirty, she's also forgetful.

"The *everyone* that you just mentioned."

She shrugs and finishes her drink, signaling for another one. "The guys in this town are jealous of you and the girls want you. That's about it."

I snort and take a sip. The liquor burns down to my stomach. That's all it does. It doesn't make me feel better, and it doesn't take my mind off Jenn.

Next to me, Miranda orders three shots and she downs them the second they appear. The bartender asks if I want anything and I shake my head. I'm still working on my second Jack and

Coke. I'm not about to get too drunk to drive my sister's car home.

Marcus would kill me if he knew I was drinking. Alcohol isn't good for an athlete's body, he'd say. He'd demand that I flush it out with a gallon of water and jog five miles to make up for it.

I take another sip. What Marcus doesn't know won't hurt him.

Miranda is talking to me, but I only half pay attention. She's talking about motocross and how her dad and brothers ride dirt bikes. She's the kind of person who can have an entire conversation by herself, so luckily it leaves me out of the obligation of talking back. I just nod every few minutes.

I check my phone but there's no new messages. It's late enough that Jenn would be off work today or out of school, or finished with whatever thing she had to do that would keep her from messaging me.

I sigh and consider sending her a text. I could ask if she wants to schedule a new fake date, or maybe keep it simple and tell her I saw something funny that reminded me of her. My finger hovers over her name on my text list, and I'm so tempted to tell her hello.

"Oh my God, you shouldn't be on your phone when you're with me!" Miranda says, shoving my arm.

At some point, she got another drink. Her eyes are glassy and she's touching my leg again. I think her barstool somehow got closer to mine as well.

She leans closer. "It's so rude to be on your phone when you're with a hot girl."

I'm about to tell her I'm not *with* her. I'm sitting *next* to her, quite out of my own control since she chose to sit next to me. But I can see in her eyes that she's drunk and I wouldn't put it past her to make a big obnoxious scene in front of everyone if I say anything that pisses her off.

"Sorry," I say, putting my phone away. "What were you talking about?"

"I was saying I give the best head," she says, blinking up at me. Her hand rises up my thigh. I put my own hand on top of hers to stop her, but she must think I'm trying to hold her hand because she grabs it and stretches out my index finger then brings it to her mouth.

I freeze, feeling one hundred percent embarrassed as she literally sucks my finger. The horrifying moment only lasts for one second, but I am mortified. What if someone saw? That's disgusting. My hands aren't even that clean.

"That's... enough," I say, trying to smile politely as I take my hand back, drying my finger on my jeans.

"There's more where that came from," she says with a drunken wink. "Let's get out of here."

"I have a busy day tomorrow." I hope she can't hear the lies in my voice. "I need to go home soon."

She frowns, then looks around the restaurant. "Ugh. You're the only hot guy here," she whines. "If you won't go home with me then how the hell am I going to piss off my boyfriend?"

Whoa.

I don't even know what to do with that information. She flicks an annoyed gaze my way and then drops some cash on the bar and reaches into her purse. She drops it, and has to pick it back up, then when she finds her keys, she drops those. She stumbles out of her stool and hits her head on the bar when bending to get her keys. This girl is a wreck.

"You're not driving home," I say. I fish some cash out from my pocket—probably way more than what my bill costs—and leave it for the bartender. I take the girl's keys and then hand her purse to her.

She looks up at me with a drunken smile and presses her finger to my chest. "Does that mean you will come home with me?" Without warning, she leans forward and runs her tongue up my neck. A literal shudder goes through me, and not the good kind.

"It means I'm taking you home," I say, pressing my hand to her back to guide her.

We weave through the packed restaurant and out to the parking lot.

"Where's your car?" I ask.

"Right here," she says, drunkenly swaying as she points to a blue SUV. "But I live over there." Her finger swings across the street to the apartment complex.

That's convenient. I can drive her home and then walk back. I help her get into her car, and she starts giggling as the alcohol takes over her inhibitions.

"I wanna suck your—" she says. I close the door so I don't have to hear the rest of it.

I get in her car and drive across the road. She points to the building that's hers, and I park, then peel her hand off my thigh again. This girl is touchy as hell.

She doesn't get out of her car on her own, and I have to walk over there and pry her out. She wraps her arms around my neck and starts kissing it, trying desperately to reach my lips. I turn my cheek away.

"Miranda," I say, forcing her away from me. "Focus. Which apartment is yours?"

Her hooded gaze smiles up at me. "I'm going to make you feel amazing," she purrs. "You'll never want to leave."

"Uh huh, sure," I say as if I'm talking to a toddler. "Show me which apartment is yours."

She starts walking and I hope she's going the right direction. Headlights pull into the darkened parking lot and then they shut off abruptly. A truck door slams and footsteps approach.

I turn around just in time to see Jay, stone-faced and bowed up.

"The hell?" he says.

Miranda gasps and then grabs onto me, wrapping her hand around my arm. "Go away," she tells him. "I found someone better."

Jay's jaw tightens. "Seriously, dude? First you steal my girlfriend then you steal my side piece?" He waves his hands through the air. "There's not any other girls in his damn town for you?"

It dawns on me in an instant. This girl is the one Jay cheated on Jenn with. This is the girl Jenn hates. And she's currently pressed up against me so much you'd think we were about to go upstairs and hook up.

I peel her off me. "I'm just getting her home safely," I say, dropping her arm.

"No he wasn't!" Miranda shouts. "He appreciates my talents and he wanted to get laid by someone who knows what she's doing."

Jay snorts. "Are you going to tell Jenn, or should I?"

I would give anything to have my wrist out of this cast so I could knock this guy into the next century. Anything. He's going to call Jenn and it doesn't matter that I had no interest in this girl, she's going to hate me.

"Look man," I say, trying to level with him. "I was just trying to do the right thing and get her home safely. She's all yours now."

Miranda reaches for me, pouting out her lips. I ignore her, toss her car keys to Jay, and start walking back toward the restaurant.

"Yeah you better walk away," Jay calls out. But he waits

until I'm pretty far away, far enough that his words are just a meaningless threat. I know he doesn't want to fight me. He's just all talk.

He's lucky because I have no words for him. I hold up my middle finger, and I don't look back.

If he tells Jenn what he saw tonight, this will all be over. But I guess if something was never actually real, it was over from the start.

EIGHTEEN

Jenn

I can't concentrate on dinner. I try so damn hard to stare at the chip bowl, to reach in and pick out one and focus on dipping it into the salsa. But I'm not really seeing it. All I see is the two of them in my peripheral vision. I glance up just as she puts her hand on his thigh. She smiles and flirts with Aiden as if it's her damn job. As if she was raised by sirens and bred into a life of flirting. She is that good at it. She's confident and sensual and everything I'm not.

I look back at the chip in my fingers.

I set it on my plate, not caring to take a bite.

"Jenn, you look awful," Mom says.

Dad stops whatever he's talking about, and now both of my parents are looking at me with concern. Great. The guy I was falling for is here with another woman and I'm here with my mom and dad like some kind of child. To make matters worse, I'm dressed like a child, too. My hair is pulled into a messy bun and I'm not wearing any makeup and if Aiden looks over here and sees me, he'll know he made the right choice with Miranda.

"I'm fine," I say, but I don't even have the energy to put fake enthusiasm in my words. It's taking everything I have not to cry.

And that makes this ball of rage swell up inside of me until I want to punch something. Rage is better than tears. I can't cry. I'm better than that.

"She's working too hard," Dad says, more to Mom than to me. "She's got the job and college and now the internship. It's too much for one person."

"You should quit working at the shop," Mom suggests.

I shoot her a look. "Are you kidding? Never. I love that place."

"Just for a little while," Mom says. She's giving me that pitying look like I really am a child again.

"You should focus more on school anyway," Dad says. "That's more important than the shop. I could find a temporary replacement for your job."

"And then I wouldn't have money for bills," I say.

Dad glances at Mom, who nods. "We can spot you some cash until the semester is over."

"Oh my god, no," I say, sinking my head into my hands. "I love my job. I'm not quitting. And I don't need money or pity from you guys, okay? I'm totally fine."

Mom's lips press together. "I just don't want school to run you ragged."

"It's not school," I say, shaking my head. "School is fine."

My parents exchange a look that in thirty years of marriage means something to them that I'll ever be able to decipher.

"Oh…" Mom says, and that pitying look seems to grow three sizes bigger. "Jay."

I roll my eyes. "No, Mom it's not Jay. I am completely over him."

"So what is it?" she says, keeping her voice low as if we're talking one on one. But I know Dad is listening. He's always listening.

"It's… nothing," I say, shaking my head. I guess it's fine if they think I'm overworked with school, because the truth is embarrassing. "Maybe I'm just tired from all the schoolwork."

Mom takes a long breath and then lets it out slowly. She puts a hand on my back. "We're here for you if you need us."

Time I find the energy to fake a smile. "Thanks, Mom."

The waiter delivers our food and my taco salad smells pretty amazing. I want to eat, I do, but I can't stop glancing over at the bar. I wonder if Aiden has seen me, but I don't think so. He's not looking around and since he's sitting at the bar, his back is to me. I stab my fork into a piece of chicken and then glance up again.

Now she's all up on him, leaning close and grabbing his hand and—*oh my God*. She just licked his finger! She put the whole thing in her mouth and pulled it out slowly like she's some kind of porn star in a competition called "Who Can Be The Biggest Skank?"

But she's not in a competition. She's in a freaking restaurant!

Who does that?

Seriously?

It's not like we're in a freaking strip club! This is a restaurant that happens to have a bar. It's not even a club. It's a family friendly place. I glance around and see all kinds of kids here with their parents. Miranda is just trashy, and there's no other explanation. I guess men like trashy.

I stare down at my food, taking a deep breath. My parents are talking about the shop and how it'll need some renovation work soon, and I nod along, like I'm paying attention. Really, all I can think about is how quickly Aiden moved on from me.

We had an amazing night together and now he's just with another girl. Like our night never existed. Like all those cuddles and hand holds and flirty texts never happened. How does a guy do that—move from one girl to the next?

A bitter, dark part of my heart laughs. I know how it happens. I know damn well how it happens.

Guys can't help themselves.

If someone offers them sex, they take it. I guess Jay wasn't a complete asshole. He gave me some valuable advice.

After a few minutes, I notice them get up and walk toward the door. Aiden seems to be guiding her because she's so drunk. Ugh. I never pictured Aiden as the type to take advantage of a drunk girl, but I've clearly been wrong about guys before. Good thing I didn't let myself fall for him. Good thing I told him we were just friends.

Good thing.

Otherwise, this pain I'm feeling in my chest might be a broken heart.

Good thing it's not.

AS THE WEEKS GO ON, I find myself thinking less and less about Aiden Strauss. It helps that I'm busy with so many other things in my life. I work as much as possible—more than I even need to —because I have this need to prove my parents wrong. Then I go to class on Tuesdays and Thursdays and take notes until my hands hurt. Then I go to PT in the evenings. I'm really loving working there, and I'm really getting the hang of working with people in rehabilitation.

I've now been trained to use the ultrasound machine which is a wand we rub over a person's injury to help it heal better. I also work with people who have had ankle fractures and get them walking again. It's so rewarding to see a patient come in wearing a walking boot and crutches and then, after a couple of weeks, they're waking without the crutches.

I know without a doubt that I want to do this for the rest of my life. On the days I intern, I stay late talking to Martha about everything her job entails. She tells me that the schooling is hard but that all the stuff you need to know becomes second nature after a while. Plus, there's yearly conferences you can travel the world to attend and they teach you about new technologies for physical therapy. It's all so cool and I'm so excited. Unlike many of my friends, I lucked out and found the perfect career for me.

Now if only I could get back on my dirt bike. I still haven't been to the track. Not in the five weeks since I walked in on Jay cheating on me. My bike is dusty in the back of the shop, which I know is a travesty to the sport. I should be keeping it clean and starting it up regularly to keep the bike maintained instead of letting it sit there and rot, but it is what it is. I just can't bring myself to ride.

I don't want to see the track, or hear the roar of bikes, or smell the exhaust. That smell used to be my favorite thing, in a weird way. I also loved the smell of race gas, but now every time a customer orders some, I see if another worker at the shop can handle it because I hate the smell. It reminds me of Jay. And then I'm reminded of how stupid I am. And then I want to throw up.

I don't even watch professional motocross on TV anymore. Even though Aiden is here in Louisiana and not racing each week with Team Loco, I still can't watch the races without being reminded of him. The TV is constantly showing the smiling faces of his teammates, and occasionally a reporter will announce that Aiden Strauss is out with an injury but should be back soon.

So now I'm not participating in my favorite sport because of Jay, and I'm not watching my favorite sport because of Aiden. Guys can really ruin everything.

Luckily, I am okay at work. I'm still fine working behind the counter and checking out customers and restocking merchandise. Every time a bike starts up out in the mechanic bay, I don't flinch or anything. These are the sounds of being at work, and I guess my brain doesn't associate it with Jay because all of that horrible shit happened at the track, not here.

I miss motocross. I do.

I miss the feel of the wind in my hair. I miss the speed and the rumble of the bike beneath me. I miss how I could pull back on the throttle and soar over a jump and feel, just for a second, that I was weightless. That nothing else mattered except for this.

There hasn't been a single time in my life where riding a dirt bike didn't fix all my problems. It's the world's best stress reliever.

But here I am, too scared to go back to the track. I'm afraid I'll cry. I'm afraid I'll run into my ex. Or my fake ex.

Or the bitch who slept with both of them.

I grit my teeth and try to shove it all out of my mind. It's Wednesday the twelfth, and it's my mom's birthday.

I'm standing in my kitchen with a bunch of cake ingredients covering my kitchen island. I pour the correct measurement of sugar into my bowl and then crack some eggs. *Focus, Jenn.*

I'm making my mom a cake like I do every year for her birthday. Then we're celebrating at my parent's house and all the extended family will come over and Dad will grill burgers and hot dogs and we'll all have a good time. It's September, but still warm enough to swim, and all my cousins will play games in the pool while the adults sip on beer and have a good time.

This is a good day. A fun day.

I will not let the thoughts of a guy ruin it for me.

I concentrate back on my cake and pour the batter into the cake pan. I grab myself a glass of wine and plop onto the couch while I wait for the cake to bake. I've already planned out how

I'm going to decorate it thanks to some Pinterest research, and I know Mom will love it.

I can't believe that a few weeks ago I had actually considered inviting Aiden to be my date to this thing. Ugh. I should have known that even a fake relationship wouldn't last this long. Apparently I'm not worth it. Apparently Miranda is better.

I down the wine and have to exert a great deal of willpower to avoid getting up for a refill. I can't be drunk at my mom's birthday party. I just can't. So I have to suck it up and deal with it. I am strong. I am independent.

I've got this.

After all, I've finally stopped flinching every time the door to the shop opens. I've stopped wondering if maybe the customer that's about to walk in the door is Aiden, because I know it won't be. I'm finally back to normal—well, mostly.

Maybe I'm finally over him.

NINETEEN

Aiden

ANOTHER DISADVANTAGE TO LIVING A LIFE OF ALWAYS traveling is that you don't exactly have a general physician. I used to see Dr. Wolff when I was a kid and lived with my mom in Orlando, but I haven't been to him in years. I rarely ever get sick, and the one time I had a cold in Colorado I swung by an urgent care center to get some medication. So after the ER doctor had put a cast on my arm and told me I needed to have it checked in six weeks, I just kind of forgot about it.

Which is why Bella and I spend all morning calling around to find a good doctor here in Louisiana. I'm tempted to fly back to Orlando and call up Dr. Wolff, but I don't want to leave my sister and grandma just yet. We've had a good time these last six weeks. When I wasn't obsessing over a girl that didn't want me, it was fun being with family. I've gotten used to Grandma's amazing cooking and it's been fun spending time with my sister now that she's practically an adult herself. Spending time here has reminded me that my whole family doesn't suck. Just my mom and older brother.

In a way, I can't believe the time has flown by so quickly. My first couple of weeks here were beyond amazing, starting with that night in the hot tub with Jenn. And then my heart was ripped out when she ghosted me. I had to learn to move on with my life and stop watching my phone for a call from her. Even now, four weeks later, I have no idea what went wrong. Did I do something? Did she move on? I know it was all fake and I know I fell a little harder than I should have but I wish she would have at least told me why she was done with me.

But I found a way to pick up the pieces of my heart and move on. It was all fake, I tell myself. I say it almost every day. Then, when I'm not lying to myself about how I'm over her, I start blaming myself. Because I could have called or texted her too. I could have put myself out there. But I can't stop thinking that maybe I obligated her into fake dating me. I was a little pushy in that hot tub. I did try my hardest to win her over. I barely even knew her but I knew I wanted to be around her. I needed more of her and maybe I pushed her into something she didn't want.

So I did the right thing for once. I stayed away. I haven't called her. Haven't texted. And she's avoided me, too. I guess this is how it is now.

My cast comes off today and I'll go back to Team Loco soon and this whole thing with Jenn will be just a memory. A sad, beautiful, too short memory.

"You excited?" Bella says, her hands gripping the steering wheel of her car that still smells like Jenn.

"Hell yeah," I say, pumping my casted arm in the air. "I'm so ready to get rid of this thing."

"I think it smells," she says, curling her lip.

She's right. It smells. Like a locker room that needs to be sanitized. I probably shouldn't have worked out so hard these past few weeks, but I had to stay in shape. No matter what, I'm going to sweat a bit and that sweat doesn't come out of a cast.

"I'll keep it and hide it under your bed so you can smell me forever," I tease.

Bella laughs. "Not happening. I'm going to ask the doctor to burn it."

We found an orthopedic doctor a couple of towns away and it takes about an hour to get to my appointment. My sister fills out my paperwork for me since it's difficult to write with my cast, and then we're finally taken back into the exam room.

"How are you feeling?" the doctor asks me when he enters the room. He's youngish, probably mid-forties.

"I'm ready to get back to work," I say.

He grins and pulls up the rolling chair to sit on it. "I understand. Casts are no fun. I hear you're an athlete?"

I nod, watching as a nurse comes into the room with a tray and the cast saw.

Bella sits straighter as the doctor turns on the saw. "Are you scared?" she asks me.

I shake my head.

The doctor chuckles. "No worries," he tells her. "There's not a blade on here." He taps the saw end to this bare forearm and nothing happens. "This piece here vibrates very quickly and that's what cuts through the cast. You might feel a little warmth, but it won't hurt."

I hold out my arm. "Let's get this over with."

The saw seems to take forever since I'm so anxious to have my arm free, but eventually the doctor cuts through both sides of my cast. He pops off the top and a rush of cool air hits my skin.

My arm is paler than the rest of me, and my arm hair is all flattened.

"How's that feel?" the doctor asks.

I hold up my arm and slowly flex my wrist. "Feels stiff, but good."

The doctor examines me and my x-rays, comparing both of my arms together. My right forearm is much smaller than the left one. Looks like I lost quite a bit of muscle.

"I'm going to prescribe two weeks of physical therapy," the doctor says after my exam. Then you'll need to see a sports doctor to determine when you can ride again. You have one of those, right?"

I nod. "There's a doctor that travels with my motocross team. He's the one in charge, I think."

"Great," he says, marking something in my file. "I'll get you that PT paperwork and you can be on your way."

"Do you know about how long it'll be before I can ride again?" I ask, desperation in my voice.

He gives me a pitying frown. "I'm afraid not. Might be a couple weeks, might be a month or two. Just take it easy for now so your bones don't get too stressed."

I nod, annoyed by his answer even though I figured he wouldn't have good news. I'm ready to get on the bike *now*. I miss it so much it hurts.

My phone rings as Bella and I are leaving the doctor's office. It's a Facetime call from Jett.

"What's up?" I say, holding the phone out in front of my face.

"Let's see it," Jett says. "Show me that naked arm."

I laugh and hold up my right arm. He lets out a low whistle. "Damn, that's a nice sight," he says jokingly. The picture blurs as he turns the phone around to where Clay and Zach are sitting in our team's motorhome. "Look at that, boys."

"Nice," the guys say.

Jett's face appears on the screen again. "So when are you cleared to ride?"

I shrug, walking slower than usual so I don't trip over something on the walk to Bella's car. The last thing I need is to break another bone. "I have two weeks of PT and then we'll see."

"That'll go by quick," Jett says.

"Says the guy who isn't banned from riding," I retort. "It's going to take forever."

"Tell him the good news," Zach calls out in the background.

Jett grins at me. "We've got this weekend off. We're coming to see you."

"No shit?" I say. Beside me, Bella looks over, eyes wide. I know she's got a huge crush on all the guys of Team Loco. "Here in Louisiana?"

"Yep," Jett says. "Clay just booked us a hotel. It's like half an hour from where you are because that tiny ass town doesn't have any hotels."

There's some noise on Jett's end and he turns the phone until I can see all three of the guys. "We're bringing a big rig," Jett says, which means a motorhome. "We're gonna hit up that local track near you, soak up the fame."

I snort. "So this is a paparazzi opportunity not a visit to see your injured friend? Dickheads."

They laugh. "We wanna see you too, baby," Zach says, blowing a kiss to the camera.

"But mostly we want to ride a local track without the pressure of a nationals race," Clay adds.

"Y'all are a bunch of assholes," I say playfully. I know they're joking around. I get off the phone and feel a thousand times better. My arm is free, my friends are coming to visit, and soon I'll be back to my normal life. Maybe I'll even forget about Jenn and finally find a way to move on from the constant dreams of what we could have had together.

OR NOT. Monday afternoon I'm sitting in the driver's seat of my sister's car, my heart thumping nervously in my chest as I stare up at the LaValle Fitness and Physical Therapy Center. I tried very hard to find a PT place that wouldn't remind me of Jenn, but this is the only one within driving distance. Damn small towns. Damn my stupid luck.

I know Jenn is just an intern and she only works here a couple days a week, so she's probably not even here. I scoured the parking lot and didn't see her truck, so that's a good sign. I'll just have to find a way to schedule all my appointments on days when she's not here. It shouldn't be too hard. I'm only supposed to have therapy three days a week, and they're open on Saturdays which is good because I know she works at the bike shop on Saturdays. I can do this. I can avoid her—at least physically.

But I don't think I'll ever be able to avoid the thoughts of her. She was my dream girl. She was beautiful and smart and stunning in every way. She had the softest skin and the sweetest smelling hair. Her lips were perfectly matched to mine. Our bodies were perfectly matched. There's no way I'll ever find someone who can compare to Jenn Doherty. There's just no way.

I stiffen and let out a sigh. I can't think like that. I can't feel the tingle in my toes when I remember how she smiled. I sure as hell can't think about her body moving in tune with mine while we reached levels of ecstasy that I hadn't thought possible. It was just one night with her, and yet it replays in my mind every night before I go to sleep.

And every time I'm in the shower.

And well, all the time.

I'm thinking of her beautiful body right now, even though I shouldn't. She doesn't belong to me. She never did. I hope she's moved on from that shitty ex-boyfriend of hers. I hope she's happy.

But most of all, I'm glad she's not here.

I walk inside and smile at the guy behind the front counter who is used to seeing me in here to work out. This time I avoid the gym section and head toward the right. I'm trying to figure out a way to coordinate my PT schedule without making myself sound like a weirdo. I can't exactly say, "Please schedule me every day that Jenn isn't here."

An older woman with cropped graying hair and purple scrubs welcomes me. She introduces herself as Martha and then goes over my paperwork with me. Standard PT stuff, which is good, she says. My broken wrist wasn't complicated, and it has healed nicely. Now I just need to get the muscles and tendons back in shape in a healthy way that won't cause further injuries.

I start to relax after a few minutes. Jenn's not here, and this will be fine. I just have to stop thinking about her.

Martha leads me behind a curtain that hangs from the ceiling. There's four separate sections like this, each with a padded table to sit on. She tells me to wait a moment and then we'll start the ultrasound.

I'm gazing off in the distance when someone walks up and pulls back the curtain. "Hello," a soft voice says. "I'm here to do your ultrasound."

My head snaps up, my heart thundering in my chest. Oh God no, this can't be happening. She hasn't seen me yet. She's looking at the paper on her clipboard. Then her eyes meet mine. She freezes.

"Hello," I say, because what the hell else should I do? Jump up and make a run for it?

Jenn takes a deep breath. "Hi."

TWENTY

Jenn

There's a lesson we're taught in school about bedside manner. If you're in a job that requires you to deal with patients, you'll occasionally come across someone you might be scared of, like a prisoner, or someone extremely sick, or maybe even a drug addict from the streets. You're supposed to be kind and supportive and treat each person like you treat anyone else. Just because they're dirty or smell bad doesn't mean you can treat them less than the human being they are. I totally agree with all of this, but...

Does the same thing apply to guys you've slept with?

I take a shuddering breath and give Aiden a polite smile. I want more than anything to turn around and tell Martha I can't handle this patient, but doing what you're told is Intern 101 stuff. I can't wimp out. I have to be a professional. Just because I know this patient in a personal capacity doesn't mean I can treat him any less than I would any other patient. So what if he slept with me and then never called me again?

Also, *dammit*. I should have known this would happen. I knew Aiden's cast would come off soon. I knew he'd need PT. I guess I assumed he'd go back to Orlando for that.

"Good afternoon," I say, staring at the paperwork on my clipboard because it's much safer than looking at him. He's gorgeous, as always. His hair has clearly been brushed but it's still sticking out all over the place. He's wearing black shorts and red T-shirt that looks sexy against his tanned skin. Now that his cast is removed, he looks sexier than ever. My brain starts conjuring up ideas of what both of his hands would feel like on my body instead of just one. I remember the rough scratching of the cast across my back. What would his touch feel like now?

Ugh. No. Stop thinking that.

"How are you?" Aiden asks. He seems just as awkward as I am right now, which is good I guess. He feels bad for ditching me. I guess that's better than if he was going to be a dick about it and point out how he doesn't like me anymore. At least he's civil.

"I'm great," I say, a little too cheerful.

Now that I'm actually paying attention to Aiden's chart, his name is written right at the top all big and prominent. Why didn't I see that before I came in here? I could have tried to prepare myself or faked getting sick so I could go home or something.

Too late now.

"I'm going to give you an ultrasound first," I say. "Then we'll do some light stretches."

"I thought ultrasounds were for seeing inside your body," Aiden says.

I pull up a rolling stool and drag the rolling cart with the ultrasound machine up to the table. "This is a different kind. It uses sound waves to heal your tissues faster."

"So there's no screen to see what the inside of my hand looks like?" he asks.

I turn on the machine and it whirrs to life. "I'm afraid not."

Now comes the most awkward part. Touching him for

fifteen minutes. "If you'd like, you can lay down," I say, gesturing to the padded table he's laying on. "Some patients prefer to since this takes a while."

He looks me right in the eye. "I'm fine sitting."

Great, I think. Of course. Continue sitting up so we're face to face. This won't be awkward at all.

I reach for his hand and he puts it in my palm. I sit straighter and pretend he is just any other patient as I squeeze the ultrasound gel on his skin.

"Ooh, it's warm," he says with a smile.

"We keep it in a warmer," I reply, keeping my gaze on his arm and *only* his arm.

I press the ultrasound wand to his wrist and begin the treatment. Basically all I have to do is run it over his skin, all around the wrist on both sides until the timer goes out. Easy. It's one of the easiest parts of being a PT intern.

Only right now it doesn't feel very easy.

I hold onto his arm with one hand and use the ultrasound wand with the other. I focus on his skin as if I need full concentration to do my job. Normally this is the part where I chat with the patient, asking small talk about their families or the weather. But with this particular patient, I am all out of things to say.

I can feel him watching me. We feel all alone here with the curtain walls closing us in, even though it's just a thin wall of fabric. I can hear Martha working with another patient, and the distant whirr of the treadmills from across the room, but still it feels like it's just me and Aiden in this place.

It's suffocating. But I don't want him to know that.

"Are you in any pain?" I ask.

"Only the pain of missing you."

My eyes flit up to Aiden's. His comment knocked the composure right off of me. He smirks in that soft, flirty way of his. My breath catches. And then the logical part of my brain speaks up.

Don't let him know how much he hurt you.

"My phone number is the same as it was a few weeks ago," I say, looking back at the ultrasound. "If you missed me so much, you could have called."

"Phones work both ways," he says softly. I'm probably mistaken, but it almost sounds like there's regret in his voice.

I shrug. "I didn't want to bother you."

"I don't think you could bother me if you tried." His voice is back to flirty.

I roll my eyes and refuse to smile. "We're friends, Aiden. You could have called me if you wanted."

"Well maybe I didn't just want to be friends," he says.

I look up.

My hardened heart is starting to crack. I can feel it. I can feel the defenses breaking down like a crumbling brick wall. I can feel that secret desire I've had ever since the day I met him rising to the surface of my heart. No. Not today.

I can't let him flirt with me like this. It's not true. He has no real feelings for me. We're just friends. That's what we agreed on, and then he proved exactly how much of friends we are by hooking up with the same girl who stole my last boyfriend.

I take a deep breath and shut down all those feelings. "I'm sure Miranda filled in for me just fine."

"What?" he flinches and my ultrasound wand slips off his arm.

I was pretty sure he hadn't seen me at the restaurant that night, but now I know for certain. I give a little shrug. "You two were pretty cozy at the bar."

Aiden's face falls, his lips pressing into a flat line.

He's been caught and it feels so good to let him know. For once, a guy didn't get to sneak around behind my back. I knew about it all along. I shrug. "That's why I didn't call. I have no desire to be friends with Miranda's guy of the week."

"Whoa, Jenn." Aiden reaches for me with his good hand, his fingertips lightly touching my arm. "That is nothing."

I snort and stare back at the ultrasound. I hate that I have to hold onto his arm to keep doing this treatment. Will these fifteen minutes ever be over?

"It's fine, Aiden. It's in the past. No need to talk about it."

"But I want to talk about it," he says, his voice getting a little louder.

I look around and then shoot him a glare. "Shh," I whisper. "Don't get me in trouble with my boss."

"Sorry," he says quietly. "But we have to talk about his, Jenn."

"There's nothing to talk about. Seriously. We're just friends so you can do whatever you want with whoever you want."

His gaze hardens. "I didn't do anything with Miranda."

"Oh that's right because sucking someone's finger is the new way of shaking hands. I forgot." I hope my sarcasm does a good job of hiding my pain.

He closes his eyes. "That girl is a mess. There's no other word for it. *She* sat by me, *she* came onto me, and *she* got so drunk that I felt bad and so I made sure she got home safely."

My jaw clenches as I work and I choose not to participate in this conversation anymore. He's probably lying, just like Jay did.

"Jenn, please," Aiden says, his voice almost a whisper. "I need you to believe me. Even if you want to keep ignoring me, I just need you to believe that one thing. Because the idea of you —or anyone—thinking I actually liked that girl makes me sick to my stomach."

I look down, my heart thundering as I work. I glance over at the ultrasound machine and it's only been seven minutes. I turn his arm over and do the inside of his wrist.

"Fine," I say. "Let's just drop it."

"I can't drop it. These last few weeks have been miserable without you."

I am smarter than this. I can't let my defenses fall, not now, not ever again. "It doesn't matter," I say, focusing on his wrist and nothing else. "Maybe I missed you too, but it doesn't matter. Your wrist is healed and you're leaving soon."

He sighs, his head falling. "I know. I just really missed you."

"I missed you too," I say. And then I get back to work.

THE NEXT DAY my classes are canceled because a transformer blew and all the power at the college went out. That's the kind of random little miracle that can really make your day. I think about going to work at my dad's shop and getting some hours in, or going back home and watching TV all night. But really, what I want to do more than anything is ride.

It's been keeping me up at night. Almost two months have passed since I've been on my bike and I'm pretty sure I haven't gone that long without riding in my entire life.

After talking to Aiden and realizing that he didn't sleep with Miranda—at least, I *think* he didn't—I'm feeling a little better. Sure, my heart still aches and I dream about a life where he didn't have to leave and we could be together for real, but I know that won't happen. Reality is that Aiden is leaving. Reality is that, yeah, we had a few great nights together. But I have to get back to my life. I can't keep avoiding the things I love because a guy ruined it for me.

So I drive to the shop and load up my bike. Rafael looks

pleased and he says he wishes he could join me but he's got to finish replacing the motor in a client's bike before the weekend.

"I'll be out there all night," I tell him as I toss my gear back in the bed of my truck. "Come out when you get off work."

He grins at me. "Sounds like a plan."

I feel jittery and excited as I drive to the track. Today is just a practice day, so anyone who wants to pay the twenty dollar fee can ride at their leisure. Tomorrow is race night, and that's a big ordeal. Hundreds of spectators will fill the stands to watch the races. Maybe I'll go tomorrow. I haven't been to a race in a while, either. It's always fun and they have really good concession stand food since the guy who runs it also owns a BBQ restaurant.

I'm feeling pumped. And so, *so* ready to get on my bike.

I drive through the gates and find a spot to park. There's a few dozen people here riding, which is a little more than usual since it's still during the day and kids are in school and people are typically at work.

I strip down to my leggings and sports bra and then pull on my protective riding gear. I strap on my boots and unload my bike and start it up, letting the motor warm up.

Then I see a group of women walking by, all giggles and gushing as they look at their phones. "Oh my god, Zach is so hot," one of them says, showing her phone to her friend.

"I think Jett is the hottest," the friend says.

I look up.

Jett? Zach? I know those names.

I look in the direction they just came from and see a small group of people huddled around a white Chevy truck. I see Aiden first. He's standing next to three other guys, smiling big to take pictures with fans. It's Team Loco in the flesh. What the hell are those guys doing here?

And furthermore, why is Aiden wearing riding gear?

I drop my gloves on my truck's tailgate and I trek over there. Aiden's eyes meet mine over the crowd of adoring fans and I crook my finger at him and say, "Can we talk?"

He excuses himself and walks over. I love the way his riding pants hang low on his hips, the way his Team Loco race jersey fits against his chest. Only after admiring him do I realize the colors are all wrong.

"Hey," he says, all smiles and good looks that make my knees want to buckle.

I grab his shoulder and turn him slightly, confirming my guess. Yep. Jett's last name is printed on the back of this jersey. "Why are you wearing Jett's gear?" I ask.

Aiden looks as guilty as a little kid who just got caught stealing from the cookie jar. "The guys came down to visit me for a few days and, well, they're gonna ride for a bit."

I put my hands on my hips. "That doesn't answer my question."

He bites down on his bottom lip and gives a little shrug. "I wanted to ride a bit. Just for fun—" he says, holding out a hand as if to stop my refusal. "Just putt around the track slowly. Just for fun."

I roll my eyes. "You can't be riding yet! Your wrist just got out of a cast one day ago."

His lips twist up into a grin. He steps a little closer and I feel my whole body tingle. "It's cute that you're worried about me."

I have the sudden urge to kiss him. And I hate myself for it.

I push him playfully in the stomach. "You should be careful."

"I'm always careful, babe."

Heat flushes to my cheeks. This can't be happening. I can't be falling for him again. It's pointless. It's reckless. It's stupid.

Aiden's playful expression turns stone cold in the blink of

an eye. I realize he's looking behind me, and I stiffen. Only one person I know has that effect on him.

"Look who's back to riding again," Jay says, a bitter laugh escaping him. I don't know if he's talking about me or Aiden, but I do know that things are about to get very uncivil around here.

TWENTY-ONE

Aiden

Jenn looks terrified. Or pissed off. I've never quite seen her like this. She turns toward that jackass who always seems to show up at the wrong time. "What are you doing here?"

He shrugs. "Just came to ride."

"Well ride somewhere else," she says, gesturing her hand toward the opposite side of the track. "You're not welcome here."

The guys on my team have been chatting with fans, but I see Jett notice Jenn and he excuses himself. I curse under my breath. I really don't want the guys to get involved with this crap. Leave it to Jett to be too friendly for his own good.

"It's a free country," Jay tells Jenn. "I'll ride wherever I want."

"No one wants you here so you should leave."

Jett walks up, giving me a huge smile. He has no idea what's going on ever here. "Hey there," he says with a wave. "I'm Jett."

He holds out a hand to Jenn, who shakes it and introduces herself.

"I'm a big fan," Jenn says. It's a little funny because most of the time when girls say that exact line, they're also freaking out and jumping up and down because they're meeting the famous Jett Adams. But not Jenn. She's calm and polite.

"Thank you so much," Jett says. He turns to Jay, also extending his hand in a friendly greeting. "Nice to meet you, man."

For a second, I worry that Jay won't shake his hand and things will get awkward, but luckily that doesn't happen.

"I'm Jay," he says, shaking Jett's hand a little harder than needed. He has a slight starstruck look in his eyes, kind of like the day he first met me. The look quickly vanishes. "I'm the winner of the series race around here."

"Oh, coql, cool," Jett says. "Congrats."

I clap my hand on Jett's back, needing to change the subject, fast. In fact, I need him to leave before Zach and Clay get curious and come over here as well. "You ready to ride?" I ask him.

Jett flashes me a grin. "I'm always ready to ride."

"I'll meet you on the track," I say.

Jett gives me a little salute and walks back to his bike. The guys brought four practice bikes from Team Loco so that we could all ride this weekend. Marcus isn't here but he gave us all explicit directions that I'm not allowed to ride if I haven't been cleared by my doctor.

I definitely haven't been cleared—but I don't care. A few slow laps won't hurt me. I even did a few pushups this morning, stopping when my wrist started hurting too bad. I know when to pace myself. I'll be fine.

Under normal circumstances, I would be completely psyched to see the guys. They're my best friends, after all, and I feel most at home when I'm with my team. But now that Jenn and I are finally talking again, I just want more time with her.

I'm so happy she's back at the track. I know that must have been hard for her to come back.

I want to hang out with her. I want to ride side by side. I want to spend time with this girl at the best place on earth—a dirt bike track.

And now Jay has showed up and ruined it all.

The temporary relief we got from Jett inserting himself in the conversation is gone now. Now it's just me, Jay, and Jenn all staring at each other. Jenn looks like she's holding back a lot of feelings. I turn to her, hoping her ex just walks away, but the opposite happens.

"I'm gonna go ride," Jenn says, turning away without so much as a look in my direction. Jay and I watch her walk back to her truck. My heart aches more with each step she takes. I turn around, planning to ignore Jay in the hope that he leaves.

But I'm not that lucky.

"You gonna tell her or am I?" Jay says. There's something extremely sinister in his voice.

I stop and turn to face him. "What are talking about?"

"I saw the way she was looking at you," he says, a grimace permanently etched on his features. "She still wants you."

"Jenn's life is none of your concern. You keep stalking her like that and I'm sure you'll have a restraining order on your hands."

"She'll be begging me to come comfort her when she learns what you did."

"I haven't done shit," I say. And it's true. All I've done is fall for the girl.

He snickers. "Guess who took a picture of you and Miranda walking back to her apartment?"

For a split second, a sliver of fear crawls up my spine. But I remember that night. I might have had my hand on her back so she wouldn't trip and fall, but I didn't do anything. It's not like he has photographic evidence of us making out, because that never happened.

"Has your life always been this pathetic or is it a new development?" I ask.

"Maybe I'll go text it to her right now," he sneers. "I'll tell her that her precious new boy toy also left her for the town slut."

I don't want him to text Jenn—not because of the photo, because I'm not worried about that. I don't want him to text her at all. She hates him. He's scum. The last thing she needs is to keep getting bothered by his dumb ass. Thoughts of finding his phone and smashing it run across my mind, but of course he'd just get a new one. Jay stares at me with this pathetic grin like he thinks he's won this round. He thinks he's scared me.

I'm not going to let him think anything of the sort.

"Jenn doesn't give a shit about you, and she already knows about the time I helped your drunk new girlfriend get back home. Oh, and just because a girl slept with you doesn't make her a slut. Stupid, maybe, but not a slut."

"Like I believe that," he spits. "You didn't tell Jenn shit."

"I tell her everything," I say. "Because I'm a real man. Not a cheater. Not a pathetic small town douche."

"Oh, you think you won her over?" he says, getting close enough for me to see the bulging vein in his forehead. "You think she's your girl now?"

I shrug as the pain of losing Jenn hits me all over again. "Doesn't matter. I'm leaving soon. Because I'm a *real* racer, not just a local champion."

My insult cuts deep—I can tell by the flinch he doesn't hide very well.

"You think you're better than me?" Jay spits.

"It's not a thought, brother. It's a fact."

"Bullshit. I'm faster than you'll ever be."

"Mmhmm," I say with a snort. "And that's why I have the sponsorship and you have a shitty small town track."

"Is that so?" Jay snaps. "Race me tomorrow. 250 Pro class."

I shrug. "Perfect."

Satisfied, Jay turns and walks away finally. I turn back to my team but they're still talking to fans and most likely haven't seen the shit that just went down. Good. Because I need to find a way to tell them I'm going to sign up for the races tomorrow.

I walk back into the group and smile big and shake hands and take some photos. I answer a ton of questions about my wrist, and assure the little kids that it doesn't hurt too bad. Clay and Zach crank up their bikes and go for a ride on the track. I notice that just about everyone gets off the track to watch them. It's a big deal, having two professional racers on a small town track.

I sit on Jett's tailgate next to him and watch our friends ride.

"So what was up with that guy?" Jett asks.

Damn, I guess he saw. I shrug. "He's the ex-boyfriend of my friend."

"Friend?" Jett says. The inflection in his voice tells me all I need to know.

I nod, ignoring his insinuation. "He's a little bitter about it. He wants her back but it's not happening. She's smarter than that."

"Is she smart enough to stay away from you?" Jett says, a smile in his words.

I chuckle, even though it's not a joke. "I hope so. I wish I could be with her but—you know how it is."

"Yeah, I do know how it is," Jett says. "You think I don't miss the hell out of Keanna right now? But I told her we wanted to go see you for a couple of days and she got excited for me and urged me to go. That's how relationships work. You make sacrifices for each other's happiness. She would have come if she could, but she's helping take care of the kids this weekend while my parents put on this massive race."

The kids he's referring to are his little sister and Keanna's little brother. Jett's parents and Keanna's parents run a pretty badass track in Texas. They're also neighbors.

"Your relationship works out because even though you travel a lot, you always come home to Keanna. You live right next to her."

He exhales. "Yeah, I guess you're right. But still—if you like this girl don't let something stupid like distance keep you apart. Besides... your grandma lives here. Maybe this place could be your home?"

I consider his words. He has a point. Breaux Valley is my sister's home, my grandma's home. Grandma has told me I have a bed at her place any time I want. What if I just settled down here in the off seasons? Could things with Jenn and me really work out?

Jett slides off the tailgate and tosses a helmet at me. "Let's go," he says. "Get on the bike and work out your thoughts."

I strap on the helmet and pull on the gloves I borrowed from Jett. It's a good thing we're the same size. I walk over to one of the practice bikes. It's decked out in Team Loco graphics but there's no number since it's not used for racing. I climb on and crank the engine, loving the way the bike sounds. I close my eyes and rev the throttle. God, I missed this. So much.

I drop it into first gear and slowly drive forward. I ride past Jenn's truck and see her sitting on her tailgate, watching me. I point at her as I drive by.

She smiles.

It makes me feel giddy—her smile mixed with the feeling of being on the bike again after all this time.

I turn onto the track and kick it up into second gear, and

then third, my right hand pinning back the throttle. I feel good. Alive. Exhilarated.

I'm supposed to take it slow, and I do for the most part, but I'm still soaring past everyone else on the track. I feel amazing on the first lap. I feel like I'm all the way back to normal. And then I go a little faster and my wrist starts to ache. I slow down a bit and shrug my shoulders. I flex my fingers. *Get it together, Aiden. You've got this.*

I approach a large jump and pin the throttle. My bike soars over it, through the air probably about fifty feet. It feels amazing, like I've flown straight into heaven. I missed this so much.

And then I land. It's a smooth landing, precise and even, but it jars the hell out of my wrist. A searing ache goes through my arm, shooting up to my shoulder socket.

Dammit.

I slow down and pull off the track, wringing out my arm. This is not what I imagined. I was hoping I was better. That maybe the doctors were just taking extra precautions. But obviously I'm not ready to ride right now.

Why did I agree to race that jackass tomorrow?

There's no way I'll let him win. But even if I tried to ride another lap right now, I know I wouldn't be able to. The pain is too much. I pull off the track and ride slowly through the pits.

When I see Jenn standing next to her truck, all of my pain seems to fade into the distance. I think about my talk with Jett. The idea of living here between races. The possibility that brings. Is there any hope in redeeming myself with this girl?

She watches me as I ride up to her truck. I stop, my feet dropping to the ground to hold the bike up. I pull off my helmet and she rushes over to me.

"How do you feel?" she asks.

I know she's talking about the wrist. But I answer a different question.

"I feel like making you my girlfriend."

Her eyes widen. "Aiden," she says, her gaze dropping to my gloved hand and then back up to me. "What are you talking about?"

I reach out and grab her with my good hand, pulling her closer while I sit on my bike. She looks so sexy in riding gear. Like a badass motocross princess. Her hair is pulled back in a ponytail that's all messy from having taken off her helmet. It's the hottest I've ever seen her.

"I'm going to kiss you now," I say, looking into her eyes for approval.

But she doesn't answer. She just leans against me and presses her lips to mine.

TWENTY-TWO

Jenn

What am I doing?

I am *kissing* Aiden Strauss.

This goes against everything I've been telling myself for four weeks. But instead of panicking about how terribly wrong this is, I'm instead thinking about how much I've wanted this again. His touch. His smell. Aiden's lips on mine.

I step closer to him. It's a little awkward because he's still straddling his dirt bike and I'm standing next to him, so we can't get as close as I'd like.

Then, he leans back and smiles at me. "Come here," he says.

He slides back on the bike seat and then pulls me to him, lifting me off the ground with the help of his newly healed wrist. Now I'm straddling the bike too, only I'm facing him, my legs going on top of his.

I wrap my arms around his neck. "People are watching us," I say softly.

"Good," he says, kissing me. "Let them stare."

I feel his strong hands hold me tightly to him and I wrap my feet around his back. I could sit like this forever, but I know the moment will end eventually, so I soak it up as long as I can.

"What are we doing?" I ask softly.

"I'm not sure what you're doing," he says, kissing me on the nose. "I'm just following my heart."

I glance back at the Team Loco truck that's several yards away. "Is this fake? Is there someone over there you're trying to trick the way we tricked Jay?"

His face falls. "No... It's just me and you, Jenn. I'm crazy about you. So terribly crazy about you. I can't stop thinking about you. I want you. I *only* want you."

My breath catches. Isn't this what I've wanted to hear, even if I tried to deny it?

"How do you want me?" I ask. Heat rises in my chest. I know I'm opening him up to an easy answer. He could say it's just sex. He could be like most guys and just say he wants me for an easy hook up.

He doesn't even hesitate before answering me.

"I want all of you. I don't want a fake version of you. I want the real you."

All around us, the sound of bikes zoom past, the heat of the day pelts down on my skin, and I'm acutely aware of all the people who are watching us. We must make quite the spectacle here, Aiden on his bike holding it up with his feet on the ground while I sit in his lap, my back against the handlebars. I try not to think about the onlookers. They don't matter. All that matters is me, and Aiden, and what happens next.

"But you were only here for six weeks," I say, looking up into his eyes. "How can we have something real if you're just going to leave?"

"It's six weeks," he says with a nod. "Or forever. You choose."

I feel a flush creep up my cheeks from the intensity of his gaze. There's something in his eyes I've never seen before, not even that time we made love. He's serious. He's fully present in the moment. He's probably not even aware of the sounds or the onlookers or the fact that it's getting really hot wearing all this riding gear and having our bodies pressed so close together. He's only looking at me. He's only *thinking* about me.

I swallow. "You would want a relationship with me even though you have a busy career?"

Aiden grins. "I'm all in, babe. I'll do whatever it takes to keep you, starting with making Breaux Valley my home."

I blink. "You're going to move here?"

He nods. "My grandma won't mind if I stay. I want to be with my sister and with you. Maybe I'll buy a house here one day, or once you graduate school we could move away somewhere more exciting together."

My eyes widen. "You've thought this through..."

His grin is so cute it makes me smile, too. He pulls me to him and kisses me on the lips. "Baby, it's all I've thought about. Every second we were faking a relationship, I was wishing it was real."

Happiness explodes inside of me. My whole body feels lighter, giddy. I bite my bottom lip and then nod. "Okay. Let's do this."

"Yeah?" he says, his eyes dancing with excitement.

"Yeah." I grab his cheeks and pull him down for another kiss.

THE NEXT MORNING is a challenge to make myself get out of bed and go to work. After riding at the track all day with Aiden, I'd kind of fallen asleep next to him in my bed. We had showered—separately—and then passed out. There was barely any time for making out because we were both so exhausted. I wake up and see him laying there, shirtless and looking sexy as hell with his messy hair, and it's all I can do not to snuggle up next to him and fall back asleep. There's so much more of him that I want to experience. I don't want to leave him, even if it is just for a few hours of work.

But I promised my dad I'd be at work today, and I'm not about to call in sick and risk having my dad find out who I brought home last night. That would just be awkward all around. This thing with Aiden is new, and it's real, but I don't want everyone to know just yet.

I slide out of bed softly, making sure Aiden doesn't wake up, and then I brush my teeth and get dressed for the day. We'd come back to my place last night after having an amazing day together. I hadn't even hesitated to invite him over. It's like now that we've moved past all of the fake stuff, we can be real with each other. I can tell him what I want and not worry about it.

I got to meet all of the guys in Team Loco and they were cool and they all seemed excited and approving of my newfound relationship with their teammate. Aiden didn't ride much because he was taking it easy on his wrist, but I rode my heart out. I went through a tank and a half of gas. I couldn't help it. It felt so good to finally be back on the bike after all these weeks of avoiding it. Eventually, Jay left and he knew better than to start any more shit with us, so that was good.

Then we all went out to dinner together and Aiden held my hand and bought my food and it dawned on me that getting dinner with his friends was our first official date. It was even better than our fake dates, which I hadn't thought possible.

I don't know how this thing with Aiden is going to work out, but I can't wait to see how it unfolds. It feels like I'm starting my life over again. Better than it ever was. I hope we can make the long distance work. I hope he doesn't get bored with me. I hope it works out.

But as I put on my socks and shoes, I remember something Jett Adams had told me last night.

"Just don't lose faith in him," he said. We were at the track, and it was one of the short times Aiden took his bike out to ride. Jett had sat next to me on the bleachers and told me he was happy for me and Aiden and all I had to do was make sure I didn't lose faith in him.

"What do you mean?" I asked.

"Professional motocross is hard," he explained. "It takes a lot out of us. But that doesn't mean he's forgotten you or he doesn't care about you anymore. So just don't lose faith in him. Be there, and be understanding. You'll find a way to make it work. I can tell that you two are perfect for each other."

"Thanks," I said, not really understanding it all.

But only now, this morning, does the weight of his words start to sink in. I am now officially dating a professional motocross racer. They have races in different cities almost every weekend. They do get a few months off between seasons, but still. It's hard. I won't see him all the time. But I'll just have to keep the faith that this can work out. If we both want it to, then it will.

At least that's what Jett had told me.

My phone lights up and I take it off the charger. I have a new message from a number I don't know.

Hɪ! It's Keanna! I hope it's okay that Jett gave me your number. :)

· · ·

I smile. Last night, Jett had told me that his girlfriend really wanted to meet me. I told him I'd like to meet her, too. He said she'd be able to give me advice about being a motocross girlfriend, and I thought that was cool. I didn't know I'd hear from her so quickly.

I reply:

Hi there! It's nice meeting you!

And then I save her number into my phone.

Keanna: I wish I could have been there this weekend but I'm busy at home. But I hope to meet you in person soon! I just had a girl's weekend with Bree, who is dating Zach and she totally wants to meet you too.

Me: That would be fun!

Keanna: Us motocross girlfriends need to stick together :) Call me if you ever need anything

I smile and thank her, and then I glance back into my room and find Aiden still sleeping. We hadn't done anything last night—besides a pretty romantic make out session—because we'd been too tired once we finally got back to my place. Now I want to crawl back into bed next to him and rekindle what we started last night, but I have to get to work.

I lean over and brush his hair away from his face. "Aiden?" I whisper.

His eyes flicker open. "Hi, beautiful," he says sleepily.

"I have to go to work, but you can stay here as long as you want."

He grins. "I'll miss you."

"I'll miss you more," I say. And then I kiss him on the cheek and head to work wearing a big ass grin on my face.

I wish I could stay, just crawl back into bed with him and never leave. But today is a race day at the local track, which means work is going to be extremely busy. I guess this will be the first of many times I have to say goodbye to Aiden when I wish I didn't.

Such is the life of a motocross girlfriend.

But so far, it's worth it.

TWENTY-THREE

Aiden

BELLA IS WAITING FOR ME ON THE FRONT PORCH WHEN I get back to Grandma's house. It's only nine-thirty in the morning, and I figured she'd still be asleep, which is the only reason I left Jenn's warm bed that smells like her. Bella stands from the porch swing and crosses her arms.

"I'm sorry I had you car all night," I say.

"I don't care about *that*," she says, making an even more annoyed face than she'd had a few minutes ago.

I jog up the three porch stairs. "Then what's wrong?"

She smacks my arm. "Jett just told me you plan on racing today!"

"Oh." I scratch my neck. "Yeah... well, it's just for fun. And how the hell have you already talked to Jett?"

"Instagram." She glares at me. "You're only on the first week of your physical therapy. You're not supposed to be riding."

I shrug. "I feel fine."

She doesn't lessen her glare. "I don't want you to get hurt again."

"I won't," I say, stepping past her and letting myself inside. Grandma's car wasn't in the driveway, so at least she's not here when Bella storms in after me, still fuming and treating me like I'm the little sibling instead of the other way around.

"I don't want you to get hurt again," she says.

"I won't get hurt," I say, handing her car keys to her. "It's just one small town race where I'll be faster than everyone else. It's just five laps. There's no competition."

Her nostrils flare. "If it's so pointless and simple then why bother doing it? You don't need to risk hurting yourself."

I shrug, seeing Jay's cocky grimace in the back of my mind. I can't back out now. "I just feel like it."

"What does Jenn think about all this?"

I stop in my tracks. Bella's eyes widen. "You haven't told her?"

I shake my head.

"Didn't you spend the night at her house?"

I'm sure I look guilty as hell right now, which actually makes my sister laugh. "Trust me, I wanted to tell her," I say. I spent all night wanting to tell her that I agreed to race tomorrow, but I knew she'd be against it and I didn't want to argue, not on the first day we decided to make this official.

I explain it to Bella, but she only looks more annoyed. "So why are you even racing? Just don't do it."

I sigh and sink into the couch, running my hand down my forehead. "Her ex-boyfriend challenged me to a race."

Bella laughs. Not sarcastically either—she's actually laughing like I'm a comedian and she's sitting in the audience having the time of her life.

Not exactly the reaction I was expecting.

She wipes her eyes. "Oh my God, what are you, like twelve? Since when do you need to race against some dickhead to prove your worth? You've been faster than small town racers since you were a kid."

I know she's right. I know I'm faster than this guy even

though I've never seen him ride. I know it shouldn't bother me and I should have just told him to piss off. But I didn't. And I can't back down now. There's no telling how many people he's already bragged about this race to. I can't be the guy who made a promise and didn't show up.

Bella frowns. "You need to tell your new girlfriend before she finds out from someone else."

"You're right," I say as my shoulders fall.

She grins. "I'm always right!"

I toss a throw pillow at her. "*Sometimes* you're right. Don't get too carried away, kid."

THIRTY SIX CYCLES is packed when I arrive an hour later. I pull my baseball cap on and try to blend in, hoping I don't become a spectacle since I'm only here to talk to my girlfriend. I make my way to the front counter and stand in line behind a woman who is purchasing a new helmet.

Jenn brightens when she sees me. "Hello, sir," she says with a cute smile on her face. "How can I help you today?"

She's so bubbly and adorable and it kills me that I'm about to say something she won't want to hear. "Can we talk for a second?" I ask, glancing around. There's no one in line right now but that could change at any moment.

Her eyes flash with worry. "It's nothing serious," I say to set her mind at ease.

"Okay," she says, motioning for me to walk around the counter to her side. "What's up? I saw the guys in here earlier."

"Did they say anything?" She doesn't seem pissed off at me, so I'm guessing they didn't tell her I'm racing today.

She tucks her hair behind her ears. "We were so busy I didn't get to talk to them. They just bought some race gas and then left."

I breathe a sigh of relief. So she doesn't know yet. "Listen..." I say, trying to formulate the words in my mind before I say them out loud. "Yesterday Jay challenged me to race him."

Her eyebrow quirks. I keep talking. "I don't know why I was stupid enough to accept it but I agreed. We're going to race today."

"Where?" she says. "Like for fun or..?"

I shake my head. "At the races..."

Her eyebrows pull together. "Like *in* the races? But you can't race. You're still healing!"

I shrug. "I don't think it'll be a big deal. I feel fine. I just can't back down, you know?"

She rolls her eyes. "I mean, you could back down. No one would care."

"I'd care," I say.

She almost looks sad for me, but I guess that's better than being pissed off like Bella was. "Okay," she says finally. "If you want to race then I can't stop you." She puts a hand on my arm. "Just be careful."

"Are you mad at me?" I ask.

She shakes her head. "Of course not. I'm here for you. I support you."

I take her face in my hands and kiss her, temporarily forgetting that we're in a store filled with customers. That her dad might be around here somewhere. I don't care. I'm crazy about this girl.

When I pull away, her cheeks are flushed pink. She grins up at me. "I guess I'll see you at the track later."

I kiss her forehead. "I can't wait."

WORD MUST HAVE GOTTEN out that three other members of Team Loco are in town, because the track is overflowing with spectators tonight. The guys are signing so many autographs I worry that they'll get carpal tunnel. I've managed to keep out of the spotlight for the most part by hanging out in the motorhome that Jett and Clay rented for the night. It's nice to have some privacy when you're stuck in the spotlight.

I'm icing my wrist and watching TV on the tiny screen in the kitchen of our rented motorhome.

Clay walks in, closing the door quickly behind him. "I miss small towns," he says, grabbing a soda from the mini fridge. "There's a certain charm to them, eh?"

"Totally," I say.

"So Jett told me about your girl," he says, sliding across from me at the little table in the kitchen. "How you're racing just to show up her ex."

I shrug. "It's pathetic. I know."

He snorts. "It's not pathetic. Guys do stupid shit to please the girls they like."

I know he's trying to be reassuring, but it doesn't help. This whole thing is stupid. My wrist has been hurting all damn day. I don't want to ride tonight. I don't care about Jay because I know without a doubt that I'd beat him in a race. But is it worth screwing up my wrist just to prove a point?

Jenn's name flashes on my phone. I nod to Clay and then answer it. "Hi babe."

"I'm here," she says. I can hear dirt bikes in the background of the phone and in real life.

"Cool, I'm in the motorhome by Jett's rental truck. We're pretty easy to find."

"Oh, I know," she says. "I'm already here."

"Cool. Come inside."

"I'd rather not."

The way her voice shakes makes me feel like shit. I had forgotten about what happened last time she walked into a motorhome. Dammit. Now I feel like the worst boyfriend ever. I rush to the door and jog outside, finding her standing next to Jett, the phone to her ear.

I lower my phone and end the call, then scoop her up in my arms. "Sorry about that," I whisper.

"It's okay," she says. But I can tell it's not. She's shaken up by the very idea of a motorhome. Screw Jay for treating her like this.

With her still in my arms, I turn around in a circle. She grins and holds onto me. "Don't drop me," she says.

"Never," I say back, kissing her just before I set her back down on the ground.

Searing pain shoots through my wrist. I can't help but wince.

"Are you okay?" she says, stepping back. "Oh my god, did I hurt you?"

"No, of course not," I say, shaking off the pain. "Damn wrist has been hurting all day."

She frowns. "Let me see."

I hold out my wrist and she takes it in her small fingers, rubbing the joint softly. I wince.

"You need to stay off it," she says. "You'll break it again, and this time it'll be a million times worse."

I can see the fear in her eyes, the worry. She doesn't want

me hurt, and I should feel the same way. I've already missed two months of motocross—and paychecks—with my team because of this injury. Is it really worth risking more just to show up some guy who doesn't matter?

"I'm not going to race," I say.

Her eyes brighten. "Really?"

I nod, sliding my hands around her waist. "It's too much of a risk."

She melts into me, laying her head against my chest. "Thank you."

I slide my fingers through her hair even though the gentle movement still hurts. I should get the ice pack and keep it iced for a while.

"Maybe we should just get out of here," I say.

She looks up at me. "Well, don't you want to hang out with the guys?"

I glance at them and shrug. "I see them all the time. I need some one on one time with my physical therapist."

"Martha?" Jenn says sarcastically. "Why do you want to be with her?"

I roll my eyes and tickle her ribcage which makes her squeal. "You know what I mean! I meant my physical therapist *intern*."

She grins. "That's more like it."

I kiss her again, letting my lips linger on hers a little longer than appropriate for being in public. She sighs, her hands pressed flat against my chest. It's all I can do not to pick her up and sneak off somewhere to make out.

When we pull away she looks just as dazed as I do. I grin. "What are you doing later tonight?"

"I'll be seeing you," she says, sliding her finger down my chest. "In the same place you slept last night."

A shiver runs through me at the very thought of being next to her in bed again. "Can we go now?"

She laughs. "We can... but I want food first. They have the best cheesy fries in the concession stand."

I put a hand to my chest, pretending that I'm wounded. "She chooses cheesy fries over me..."

"Hell yeah I do," Jenn says playfully as she slips her fingers into mine and leads the way to the concessions. "You taste good and all, but you provide no sustenance whatsoever."

I love when she's in a playful mood like this. It's so much nicer than seeing the pain that lingered behind her eyes those first few times we hung out. As we walk through the crowds of people, it feels like nothing could kill my happiness right now. Not until Jay steps out in front of us, when we're just a few steps away from the concession stand.

"Ready to lose to a local racer?" he snarls. I grip Jenn's hand tightly in mine. I can feel her whole body tense up at seeing her ex. I step forward a bit, shielding her body from his view. "I'm not gonna race you, man."

Jay's brows shoot up his forehead. "You're seriously going to back out?"

I shrug.

It occurs me now that I don't have anything to prove to him. Jay is an egotistical meat head who fights with his fists, not his brain. He spends his whole life trying to be better than everyone else, and for what? To make himself feel better. This is the kind of weak man that Jenn wasted years of her life on. She deserves so much better.

So even as Jay continues to insult me, tightening his fists at his sides like he's two seconds away from throwing the first punch, I just shrug and take a step back.

"I'm not gonna fight you."

I glance at Jenn who is watching the scene unfold with a terrifying look in her eyes. I squeeze her hand and turn back to face Jay.

"You can tell the whole world whatever you want to tell them, but I don't need to beat you in a race to prove that I'm the better man. I've already done that."

TWENTY-FOUR

Jenn

M_Y CHEESY FRIES TASTE EVEN BETTER THAN USUAL tonight. Or maybe it's just my extraordinarily good mood that's making everything better. The sun setting in the sky is more beautiful than I remember. The sound of dirt bikes on the track is like music to my ears. And the smell of Aiden's cologne while he sits next to me on the bleachers must have some kind of magical powers because all I want to do is snuggle against him.

We're already sitting close. My leg is up against his while we hang out near the top of the large metal bleachers that overlook the track. The races have begun, but we're only a couple motos in to what will be a long night with at least twenty six different races. They're separated out by ages and size of bikes. Right now the little kids are on the track, their tiny bikes barely making a sound as they cruise around slowly.

Aiden leans over and steals one of my cheesy fries. "These things are good."

"I told you," I say, taking another bite.

One girl walks up the bleachers, smiling at Aiden as he passes. He gives her a polite nod. When I was with Jay, I would get jealous of things like this, because it was always initiated by him. He flirted with girls all the time. But it's different with Aiden. He's a celebrity around here and people are drawn to him. He's just being nice. His gaze doesn't linger on the girl, and he doesn't turn around to check out her ass like Jay would have done.

Being with Aiden makes me wonder how I ever put up with Jay in the first place. Aiden and I finish off my cheese fries, and suddenly there's no reason for me to be here anymore.

"You wanna get out of here?" I ask.

The bright lights overhead make his eyes sparkle as they narrow at me. "I thought you'd never ask."

As SOON AS we get into my apartment, I shove the door closed behind us and lock it. I toss my truck keys on the table and then throw my arms around Aiden's neck.

He chuckles as I lean against him, my fingers sliding through his hair. "What's this for?" he asks, his hands sending a shiver down my spine as they slowly move down my sides, stopping on my hips.

"I just really like you," I say, gazing into his eyes. "How you handled Jay tonight... that was really great of you. It was sexy."

He quirks an eyebrow. "Oh yeah?"

I lean up on my toes and kiss him quickly. "It was *really* sexy. I like that you don't have to act all macho."

He shrugs. "I'm macho where it counts."

"Oh yeah?" I say, poking him playfully in the chest. "And where does it count?"

"Right now," he says, faking a caveman type voice. His

hands slide under my butt and he pulls me toward him, then he lifts me off my feet, wrapping my legs around his waist.

I see him wince the second he does it, probably because his wrist shouldn't be picking up fully grown women, but he tries to hide it.

I shimmy out of his arms. "Babe... your wrist is hurt. Stop picking me up."

"I'm fine," he says, but he's holding his wrist now and his brows are pulled together, creasing his forehead. "Seriously. I'm fine. What kind of guy can't pick up his own girlfriend?"

I roll my eyes. "A guy who just got his cast off. You big dork."

I point to the couch. "Go sit down."

He groans in protest and steps toward me until my back is against the wall. His good hand grabs my hip as he crushes his body against mine, his other elbow resting on the wall near my head.

"I don't want to go to the couch," he says, his voice a near growl in my ear. Heat rises up through my belly as he kisses my neck so softly that I barely feel it. "I want to go to the bed," he whispers, his lips grazing my skin.

My breath catches. He kisses my neck, sending a trail of heat across my skin until he reaches my mouth. Our lips move urgently, passionately, our tongues finding each other.

Then I slowly pull away. The physical therapist in me is still worried about his wrist. "We have all night," I say, giving him a look that I hope he understands as sincere. "Right now we need to take care of your wrist."

He pouts out his bottom lip and I lean up on my toes and kiss it. "Go sit on the couch," I say. "I'll be right back."

He does as he's told, and I grab the jar of emu oil from my medicine cabinet. This stuff works wonders on pain.

He's sitting on my couch with his legs stretched out across it. I nudge his leg with my knee. "Move over."

He gives me a devilish grin and opens his legs, patting to the space between them. I roll my eyes and settle myself on the couch, my back against his chest. This looks a lot like cuddling instead of therapy, but when he leans forward, brushing my hair over one shoulder, and kisses my neck, I suddenly have no objections.

"Give me your hand," I say, my voice weak.

I take his wrist and rub the emu oil on it. Then I work my thumbs gently around it, massaging the tendons from his palm to his forearm.

His kisses stop momentarily and he sighs. "That feels amazing," he says.

I glance back and grin. "Good."

He kisses my cheek. I turn my attention back to his hand. His good hand holds onto my thigh, and it slowly creeps up higher to places that make my whole body tingle. I concentrate on his injury though, massaging it the way I've been taught in school.

After several minutes, Aiden's good hand slides up even further, cupping my breast. His lips press to the back of my neck and I freeze, unable to concentrate on anything but the glorious feeling of his skin on mine. I feel his chest muscles flex as he leans forward, pressing us closer, his hand holding my breast while his lips trail kisses around to my shoulder and then collarbone. I hold his injured hand in both of mine, caught halfway between massaging it and wanting to close my eyes and take in Aiden's gentle caresses.

I draw in a shuddering breath. "Okay. Therapy is over," I say, letting go of his hand. I turn around so that I'm facing him, straddling his legs on the couch.

His tongue flicks across his lips and the smile he gives me

is filled with naughty thoughts. I narrow my eyes and lean into him, kissing him hungrily while our bodies grind together. I want to rip his clothes off. But I also want to take my time.

I want to enjoy every moment with him.

"Baby," he says, his lips still pressed to mine.

"Yeah?" I say back, lifting my head a little so I can look at him.

"Promise me this is going to work."

There's a seriousness in his eyes that takes me out of my love-drunk moment. I blink. "What do you mean?"

"Us," he says, his eyes roaming my face. "I've never felt this way about anyone, and I'm scared to death that I'll lose you. We have a long journey ahead of us and I can't lose you. I can't."

I shake my head and silence him with a kiss. "You're not going to lose me."

"What about the long distance? The traveling?"

I shrug. "We'll figure it out."

He closes his eyes briefly, inhaling a deep breath. "You have no idea how much you mean to me."

I smile. "The feeling is mutual. Trust me."

He reaches up, his fingers grazing my cheek. "This is real."

It's not a question. More like he's saying it to reassure himself. I can't lie—there's worries in my mind as well, but I know that I want him more than I've ever wanted anything in my life.

"It works for Jett and Keanna," I say. "And Zach and Bree. It'll work for us."

He pulls my head down and kisses my forehead. With his lips still pressed to my skin, he murmurs, "I love you. You don't have to say it back yet, but I do. I love you so much."

I look up and feel a warmth spread through my entire body. I know I don't have to say it back, and all the reasons why come flying at me—it's too soon, it's a big commitment, it's scary as hell.

But none of those reasons matter, because nothing has ever been so true in my entire life.

I look him right in the eyes. "I love you, too."

ABOUT THE AUTHOR

Amy Sparling is the bestselling author of books for teens and the teens at heart. She lives on the coast of Texas with her family, her spoiled rotten pets, and a huge pile of books. She graduated with a degree in English and has worked at a bookstore, coffee shop, and a fashion boutique. Her fashion skills aren't the best, but luckily she turned her love of coffee and books into a writing career that means she can work in her pajamas. Her favorite things are coffee, book boyfriends, and Netflix binges.

She's always loved reading books from R. L. Stine's Fear Street series, to The Baby Sitter's Club series by Ann, Martin, and of course, Twilight. She started writing her own books in 2010 and now publishes several books a year. Amy loves getting messages from her readers and responds to every single one! Connect with her on one of the links below.

www.AmySparling.com